For a moment ~~their hands~~
locked,

and then they both turned to look out across
the sea. Tom moved his hand along the rail
away from hers.

Fee took several deep breaths and tried to
shake away the peculiar feeling the feather-
light touch of his finger had produced.
Nothing like this should happen to her.
Sensible, practical Nurse McFie. Certainly not
with Tom Cameron, whom she didn't even
like.

She was clearing her throat to say something
when Tom spoke again, picking up from
where he'd left off as if nothing had
happened. Nothing *has* happened, she assured
herself.

Margaret O'Neill started scribbling at four and began nursing at twenty. She contracted TB and, when recovered, did her British Tuberculosis Association nursing training before general training at the Royal Portsmouth Hospital. She married, had two children, and with her late husband she owned and managed several nursing homes. Now retired and living in Sussex, she still has many nursing contacts. Her husband would have been delighted to see her books in print.

Recent titles by the same author:

A NURSE TO TRUST
THE GENTLE TOUCH

DOCTOR IN NEED

BY
MARGARET O'NEILL

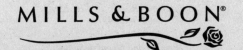
MILLS & BOON®

To Chris, without whom…

*First published in Great Britain 2002
Harlequin Mills & Boon Limited,
Eton House, 18-24 Paradise Road, Richmond, Surrey TW9 1SR*

© Margaret O'Neill 2002

ISBN 0 263 83061 6

*Set in Times Roman 10½ on 12 pt.
03-0402-49733*

*Printed and bound in Spain
by Litografía Rosés, S.A., Barcelona*

CHAPTER ONE

FEE drove at a snail's pace along the empty coast road that encircled the island. It was too hot to hurry and she only had one more patient to see before lunch. The windows of the Land Rover were wide open to catch whatever breeze there was coming in off the sea. She turned her head to look out over the blue-green, glittering water of the Sound of Drummock, and gave a sigh of contentment.

'Count your blessings, Fiona McFie,' she murmured. 'You're a lucky woman to live and work in a place like this.'

She turned back to look straight ahead, where the road curved gently, following the line of the coast. Just round the bend a large camper van was pulled into a passing place, but it still nearly blocked the already narrow road.

Fee slowed almost to a stop, prepared to edge past the vehicle. A blond-haired man leaned out of the driver's window as Fee drew level.

'Sorry about this,' he said. 'Do you think that you can make it?'

He had a nice voice, Fee thought—melodious, slightly husky, with a trace of a Scottish burr overlaying an English public school accent. He had very blue eyes, fringed with dark blond lashes that any woman would die for.

'I stopped to give the kids a chance to stretch their legs,' he explained, waving toward the small bay of jumbled rocks and sand where a boy and a girl in shorts

5

were racing in and out of the water. Fair-haired like their father—presumably he was their father—they looked lightly tanned and fit. The girl was a little plump, the boy was rake-thin as only young boys could be. They were wearing baseball caps with the brims over their necks.

'I hope that they're wearing plenty of sun cream,' said Fee.

The man pretended to scowl and rolled his eyes dramatically. 'Sun cream,' he muttered, 'has cost me a fortune this holiday. Think I'll take my next one in midwinter, preferably in the Arctic Circle.'

'Better to be safe than sorry,' Fee smiled, easing the car forward. 'Enjoy your stay on Drummock.'

'By the way,' he said, as she began to move off, 'can you direct me to Quay House? I know that it's down near the harbour, but it's donkey's years since I was here and I seemed to have missed the turning when we came off the ferry.'

Fee frowned, switching off her engine. 'Yes, I can direct you, but you won't find anyone there. It's the doctor's house—that is, when we had a doctor, which hasn't been for some time. Perhaps I can help. I'm the district nurse amongst other things, and pretty fair with a bandage or injection, and I can write up certain prescriptions. What can I do for you?'

His eyebrows shot up again, the eyes registered surprise. 'The district nurse? You're not in uniform. And what do you mean, ''amongst other things''?'

Did he mind her not being in uniform? With his casual mop of flaxen hair he didn't look as if he would mind. On the contrary, he looked as if he might be rather easygoing. Well, why not? He appeared to be on holiday, so what he thought of her sartorial appearance didn't matter a hoot. It was up to her whether she wore a uniform. She was her own boss.

She wasn't sure whether she was imagining it, but was there a change in his voice? Surely, it was crisper, rather authoritative. But why on earth should a visitor be *that* interested in her? Not that it mattered. Her life was an open book.

The thoughts sped through her head as she looked across at him. They were separated by only a few inches. His eyes were incredible pools of deep blue, beautiful but shrewd.

'I'm also a midwife and health visitor,' she said, 'and have a qualification as a registered nurse general practitioner covering these specialities and a few more besides. At the moment, I'm acting as locum to the non-existent resident doctor, with a little help from the mainland medics. And, as I said, I can write a certain range of prescriptions.' Well, he'd wanted to know who and what she was, and she'd told him. 'Almost as good as the real thing,' she added with a grin.

The stranger raised expressive eyebrows. 'Ah, yes, Miss Fiona McFie. I've heard of you. I'm afraid that I've jumped the gun rather by arriving early. I'm the new doctor—Thomas Cameron.' He stuck his hand through the open window.

Fee stared at him speechlessly. After a moment he withdrew his hand. 'If you don't believe me, I've got the letter offering me the job here somewhere...' He rummaged on the seat beside him for a moment, then turned back to her and held up the document for her to see.

Fee's eyes scanned it incredulously. They'd appointed a new doctor without telling her!

'Look, obviously this has come as a bit of a surprise,'

he said. 'It's true I've arrived early, but I wanted the children to get acclimatised before I start work. I'm sure you'll receive the official notification soon. I'm sorry not to have met you before, but I've been abroad until recently, and was unable to get here any sooner. I assumed you knew I was coming. Your position on Drummock was explained to me when I applied for the job. I understand that the chairman of the island hospital trust—Ian McKay, I believe—is away at present, but I was told his approval of my appointment was a formality. Drummock having been without a doctor for so long, his endorsement was taken for granted.'

He watched as a range of expressions flitted across Fee's face and regretted that final remark. Obviously she was feeling deeply upset about the whole thing.

He added lamely, 'I take it you haven't heard anything about any of this?'

Fee could only shake her head.

'Then I must apologise. Partly my fault for arriving early. I don't officially start for another ten days, but Dr Maybury thought that it would be in order if I came over to look around. He said I could stay at Quay House as we haven't any accommodation fixed.' He shrugged. 'And here we are.'

That was typical of the arrogant Dr Maybury, Fee thought.

'Yes, here you are,' she said aloud. She was recovering her cool, but she couldn't stomach much more of this. She needed time to think. 'And what our esteemed medical officer of health says, goes.' She started her engine again. 'To reach Quay House you continue along the coast road for a mile or so, and then turn for the township. Take the lower road and you can't miss it. Goodbye, Dr Cameron. Inevitably we will soon be meeting again in an official capacity.' And slipping the car into gear, she drove off.

She tried to marshal her thoughts as she drove. It wasn't possible to tell a newcomer that the mainland medical authorities sometimes treated the islanders as second-class citizens. How to explain the sort of uneasy truce that existed between her and the mainland authorities?

There were officials, both medical and administrative, who resented her position on the island. Some older doctors in particular thought she shouldn't have so much medical responsibility. Not that they were prepared to come over and take her place, of course. But while her friends and relations might be free to comment on this, it wasn't the place of a stranger to become embroiled in the business.

Outwardly calm, inside she was fuming. Her temper and blood pressure were rising and simultaneously her breathing was getting almost to the point of hyperventilation. So that was all the thanks she got for holding the fort for three overworked months! Not even the courtesy of a phone call to say that a doctor had been found. If only Ian hadn't been away, none of this would have happened. He would have made sure that they all had a chance to size up this Dr Cameron first, not simply accept the authorities' decision.

How could they treat her—and Drummock—so shabbily?

And why had this Dr Cameron arrived so early, trailing his family with him? He'd implied that he'd visited Drummock some time in the past, but had that been enough to convince him he should take up a position here? He was obviously not that familiar with the island. It all seemed unusually hasty. For that matter, if he had

children, was there a wife in tow somewhere? Perhaps
she would be turning up later.

Fee gritted her teeth, and took some more deep
breaths. She had to keep her cool for another half-hour
or so while she saw her last patient. After that…

'All hell will break loose,' she spat out aloud, gripping
the steering-wheel until her knuckles turned white.
'Those smart types on Skleet won't know what's hit
them.'

Her patient, Roddy Douglas, an elderly widower,
lived a mile further along the coast, tucked just inside
The Windings. The Windings was a long narrow lane
that wove its way to the middle of the island and the
foot of Ben Drummock. The mountain, small as mountains went but rugged enough to attract climbers, dom-
inated the landscape.

Roddy had only returned the day before from hospital
on the mainland where he'd been operated on for an
enlarged prostate gland. At the moment Fee didn't know
why his prostate was enlarged—that information hadn't
come back with him. The letter from the hospital had
simply said that in addition to removing the prostate, the
surgeon had also performed a small investigative laparotomy.

But a laparotomy to investigate what? wondered Fee.

Roddy Douglas was a grumpy old man and shy of
young women, so he probably wouldn't let her examine
him to see if everything was looking normal. However,
she particularly wanted to check the laparotomy wound,
which would hopefully be fairly minor.

'My private parts are my own business,' he'd told Fee
when she'd visited him a fortnight ago when a neighbour
had called her in because he was 'not too bonny'.

So she would have to do now what she'd had to do

then, when by question and answer she had diagnosed him well enough to arrange for his admission to St Catherine's.

His front door was on the latch. Fee tapped and pushed it open, calling out as she did so. 'Roddy, it's me—Fee McFie, the nurse.'

'Then I suppose you'd better enter,' grumbled the old man. 'Though I didna ask you to come.'

In spite of the outside temperature being in the seventies, there was a fire going in the tiny sitting room. Roddy was sitting with his slippers almost in the grate and a rug over his knees.

The wall of heat hit Fee and she left the door to the hall open as she moved into the room.

'And you can close the door behind you,' muttered Roddy.

Reluctantly Fee pushed the door to and crossed over to him.

'The hospital asked me to visit you, Mr Douglas,' she said formally, since being friendly wasn't getting her anywhere. 'I need to check that the site of the operation is clean and healing properly and is not causing any problems.'

'It's not,' said the old man curtly. 'It's doing just fine. You don't have to check it—just take my word for it.'

'Any swelling or soreness?'

He glared at her. 'I told you, it's all right, though they butchered me over there.' He jerked his head toward the mainland. 'They didn't just take out "the thing" but they cut open my belly.'

Fee ignored the remark about butchering but asked the old man how the scar felt where they'd cut him. 'It isn't a very big one, is it?' she half questioned, half suggested. With so many ways of investigating these days by scanning and keyhole surgery, surgical laparotomies were getting rare.

'It's big enough,' grumbled the old man, 'but you don't have to concern yourself with that. It's all healing up fair enough.'

Fee nodded. She would have to phone the hospital later in the day to find out why they had performed a laparotomy, and if possible winkle out any more details she could out of them. The trouble was that some of the doctors on the mainland were reluctant to pass on certain information to anyone but another doctor. Although, with her qualifications, they shouldn't be so reticent. Anyway, who could they report to but her while there was no resident doctor on Drummock?

But there is now!

The disturbing fact sat there in the back of her mind, bitter and shaming.

She shook off the pall of gloom, and made herself concentrate on Roddy. But she could feel her patience, already stretched since her meeting with Thomas Cameron, growing thinner in the excessive heat.

'But you're not having problems passing water now, are you? That was jolly painful, if you recall, so you should be grateful to them for fixing that.'

Roddy Douglas grunted noncommittally and Fee gave a resigned sigh.

'Very well. I won't trouble you any further, then,' she told him, moving to the door. 'But you should be grateful to Mrs Fraser next door. If she hadn't phoned me you would have been in real trouble by now. She's a saint, the way she looks after you, and you should appreciate her more than you do. I'll call in again at the end of the week unless you need me before, Mr Douglas. Goodbye.'

Once outside Fee leaned against the wall beside the front door and took in more deep breaths. Douglas was a testy old man but she shouldn't have let her temper get the better of her like that. It's bad nursing practice, she told herself, to lose one's cool with a patient. The poor old thing might need chemotherapy if the enlargement was due to cancer, and that would mean frequent trips to the mainland and possibly unpleasant side effects from the treatment.

She drove home for lunch, her mind a maelstrom of unhappy, bitter thoughts. Why had the admin people on the mainland not informed her immediately that they had found a doctor for Drummock? Was there some old boy network operating? Had Dr Cameron been appointed without applying through the usual channels?

But if that were true, why keep it secret from her of all people? They must have some idea of the workload she'd been carrying and know that she would welcome more help. They had been anxious enough to encourage her when the old doctor had first retired, reassuring her that if she could hold the fort for a while they'd soon find a replacement.

Three possible applicants had turned up in those first weeks, two men and a woman. One of the men had been a surfing addict who'd thought that Drummock's surf beach, mentioned as an inducement in the advert for a doctor, a joke. He hadn't wanted to know anything about the practice on the island and couldn't wait to get the next ferry back to the mainland.

'And good riddance to you,' Fee had muttered to his retreating back as he had hurried on to the ferry. She would have liked to have thumbed her nose but had decided that he hadn't been worth such an undignified gesture. Some doctor!

The other male medic was in his sixties and not far off retirement. Neither he nor the administrative officer who had escorted him seemed to know what he was looking for but, whatever it was, he didn't find it on Drummock. He was very courteous, and thanked Fee for putting him in the picture regarding the practice.

'But I don't think it's quite...' he began, then trailed off, shrugged regretfully, and was never heard of again.

The woman doctor was the most promising. Fee liked her at once. She was in her early thirties, had holidayed on Drummock when a child and seemed not in the least daunted by the size of the practice she would be expected to manage. She wasn't married or in a relationship with anyone. Her CV was excellent. She could start work in August. Great! Only she never showed up and couldn't be traced.

None of the referees existed or, if they did, they knew nothing about her. Her CV was a fabrication. The hospitals she had supposedly worked in had no record of her ever being employed by them. She was a complete sham.

Fee pulled up outside her house with a squeal of brakes, very unlike her usual neat manner of parking. She sat in the hot vehicle staring straight ahead.

Well, at least she knew Thomas Cameron wasn't another sham. He at least had produced documents to show he'd been officially appointed. But why hadn't the authorities had the common courtesy to inform her that the vacant post had been filled? For that matter, why hadn't she been given the opportunity to vet the candidate first? Did they think that little of her, or were they so grateful to fill the post that they'd accepted the first half-decent applicant?

It would be just like the authorities to do that.

'The authorities' was a general term used on Drummock to encompass any mainland board, institution or official body. Usually it was employed in a disparaging or sometimes downright contemptuous sense. In the same way 'the mainland' was used to describe almost anywhere that wasn't Drummock. They were a close-knit community who did things their own way. And now they had a stranger in their midst.

No! She wouldn't phone the authorities yet, Fee decided. She would wait until she had more facts to back up her anger which was currently at boiling point; wait until she could think rationally and calmly. Meanwhile she would make her own mind up about Dr Thomas Cameron.

Both her mobile and her house phone were ringing as she opened the door to her flat. She answered the mobile first.

'Fee McFie!' said a shrill, angry voice, thick with the local accent. 'You might at least have had the courtesy to tell me that the new man was arriving so that I could give the place a proper clean, instead of letting me find him and those puir wee bairns on the doorstep...' Maggie Shillington, the housekeeper of Quay House, whose temper at best was of the switchback variety, paused for breath.

Fee leapt into the pause. 'Maggie, stop! I presume you mean the new doctor?' Not waiting for a reply, she added quickly, 'I didn't know he was coming! Nobody informed me either.'

There was a snort of disbelief from Maggie.

'Well, think what you like, Maggie, but I promise you it's true,' Fee said, and rang off before Maggie could make further comment or she herself could be indiscreet about the new doctor and the anger it had stirred up inside her.

The house phone was still ringing and she picked up the receiver. 'Nurse McFie,' she announced briskly. 'How can I help you?'

'By agreeing to meet me to clear up a problem that should never have arisen,' replied Thomas Cameron in his well-modulated English voice, overlaid with a touch of brogue.

His voice stirred up her anger still more. She had to wait until her heartbeats slowed down before she could answer in what she hoped would be a normal voice.

'I suppose Maggie gave you my number,' she said by way of reply.

'No, I'm in the study of Quay House and your name and phone number are written large on a wall pad, with a note, presumably by my predecessor, saying, ''When in doubt, ring Fee.'' So I'm ringing you. May I call and see you, or would you rather come and see me? I'm easy either way.'

Should she see him, or should she wait until the authorities had the grace to notify her of his presence? But supposing they didn't? Supposing that they simply heaved a sigh of relief at having covered themselves by appointing a doctor and left it to her to get on with it? A few hours ago she wouldn't have given the possibility a second thought, but disillusionment had now hit her and she was discovering just how indifferent the admin people seemed to be to her situation.

'The problem is not of my making, Dr Cameron,' she said curtly.

'Nor mine.' He was just as curt. 'But surely we can be civilised even if the powers that be don't know their manners and fail to come up to scratch. After all, it's in our own interests to lay the foundations of a friendly relationship. We'll be working together for a long time to come.'

'I wonder,' whispered Fee bleakly half to herself. Pulling herself together, she added in her normal voice, 'You'd better come to me. I'm only just down the road from Quay House. I've got a surgery at two at the hospital, and I'll have to start promptly.'

'I'll set off as soon as Maggie Shillington comes back,' he said. 'She's gone to fetch a casserole. She thinks my kids are starving to death because they haven't had a hot meal today.'

'Maggie would,' Fee said, and put the receiver down.

She made herself a salad sandwich washed down with ice-cold lemon squash, made by Mary Mackintosh her neighbour in the flat below hers. Mary, widowed when her husband, a fisherman and lifeboat man, had died, was a bit smothering at times, but a good friend and a welcoming sight when Fee came home on a winter's evening after a long hard day.

'Come in for a wee dram,' she would insist. 'You need it and it'll give me an excuse to have one, too. Like Alistair used to say, before the silly old fool got himself drowned, as a body gets older you need your creature comforts.' Usually she blew her nose hard at this point. She always referred to her late husband as 'that silly old fool', the loving tone of her voice belying her words.

Fee sat outside on the little balcony at the top of the circular iron staircase, shaded by a potted palm tree which she had nurtured since it was a few feet high. Now it was just tall enough to provide a little shade.

The harbour was, as always, bustling. A ferry had just come in, disgorging visitors and residents returning to the island. The Indian summer weather had brought a number of late holidaymakers who wouldn't normally have ventured out to Drummock this late in the year.

About the harbour was the town of Drummock, the only settlement of any size on the island. It was an assembly of low, solid houses, mostly of grey stone, but with a few here and there adventurously picked out in white or pastel-coloured rendering. Beyond the town were rolling green hills, pierced by occasional crags and outcrops of rock, and cut through by narrow valleys sheltering copses of low, wind-twisted trees.

It was a familiar sight which she normally loved to look upon, but this afternoon it hardly registered. Her mind was too full of the latest unexpected turn of events. How was she going to sort things out...?

Cameron's voice suddenly hailed her from the foot of the spiral staircase, breaking into her reverie. 'May I come up?'

His presence seemed to rekindle the fires of her resentment. Not trusting words, she simply nodded and waved to him to come up.

She'd seen that he was a large man even when he'd been sitting in the camper van, but now, watching him come up the stairs two at a time, his flaxen hair gleaming in the sunshine, she saw that he was six feet four or five. He was wearing shorts and his thigh and calf muscles were taut and firm. Fine hairs, fair against the bronze of his legs, seemed to emphasise their strength.

Where on earth had he been practising medicine? Some glamorous Californian resort perhaps, or somewhere on the French Riviera or Australia? He looked as if he might have come from the outback, all tough and laid back.

Fee snapped out of her review of his physical attributes and rose from the low garden chair.

'Please, don't get up on my account,' he said.

'I'm not,' she replied crisply, not meaning to sound rude but finding it difficult to talk to him. 'There's not room for us both out here, and we're in full view of the world and his wife and will be subject to interruptions. We'll go inside to talk.'

She brought the jug of still chilled lemonade in with her, and offered him a glass. They sat in cane chairs at the round cane table in the kitchen. The room was relatively cool, with a big old-fashioned fan turning slowly just beneath the ceiling. The very tall windows were wide open, facing away from the sound and looking across the interior of the island to Ben Drummock.

It was a fascinating room, the proportions extraordinary, and Tom Cameron would have liked to have asked about its history, but one look at Fee's face told him that wouldn't be a good idea.

'So,' Fee said, 'what do you want to talk about, Dr Cameron?'

He took a long swallow of lemonade. 'I want to clear the air between us. You seem to think that I colluded in keeping you in the dark about my appointment. Well, I didn't and I have no idea why the people on the mainland didn't make it clear just how much you've obviously been doing here.'

'Weren't you curious to know who had been looking after the Drummock residents—diagnosing, prescribing, arranging for X-rays and other tests?' Fee retorted. 'We islanders are a pretty healthy bunch but we're not entirely immune to life's little ills. Women still have babies, old people have falls or get pneumonia. Didn't you wonder who had been looking after things since the old doctor retired?'

Fee couldn't keep the hurt and bitterness out of her voice.

Tom met her eyes across the table and saw the contempt in their sea-green depths. He knew then that this woman was going to take a hell of a lot of convincing that he wasn't as superficial and uncaring as he must seem to her.

'I understood, from the medics and other people I talked to on the mainland, that a doctor visited regularly and could be contacted by phone or e-mail whenever necessary.'

Even to his own ears, it sounded more of an excuse than a reason. Why the devil hadn't he asked more questions and insisted on being put in touch with 'the capable senior nurse who manages the nursing side of things', as she had been casually referred to, before he arrived? Just one phone call might have avoided this confrontation.

Perhaps he'd just been so grateful to find somewhere that appeared to offer a home and a job where both he and, more important, the children could be safe and happy. They all needed that after the awful year just behind them. But without going into those events in depth—and he wasn't prepared to do that yet by a long chalk—it would simply sound like a sob story to Fiona McFie, trundled out to excuse his shortcomings.

Fiona was still fuming. 'Didn't it occur to you to ask who was capable of deciding when it was necessary to contact a doctor?'

Tom shook his head. 'No, I'm sorry, it didn't. I hadn't come across a situation like this before. All I can do is apologise for in any way having ignored you and your professional contribution, and hope that we can work together in the future. I'll be relying on you to steer me in the right direction until I find my feet.'

For the second time that day he held out his hand to shake hers. This time, after a momentary pause, Fee took it.

'Welcome to Drummock, Dr Cameron,' she said, as she placed her hand into his.

But there wasn't much warmth in her voice, Tom thought with a mixture of regret and irritation. He couldn't think what else he might do by way of an apology. Perhaps when he actually started work, he would make more progress.

He stood up. 'Thank you for the lemonade, Nurse McFie—or should it be Sister McFie?'

For the first time, Fee almost, but not quite, smiled at him. 'To most of the residents who have known me since I was born, I'm generally known as Fee. Nobody would recognise me as Sister anything. Nurse is good enough for them and for me, thank you, Doctor.'

Another snub. Tom thought that she was itching to add something like 'coming from the city with your fancy ways as you do'. But that may have been his imagination working overtime. He shrugged mentally. Well, he'd done what he could. All he could do now was hope that time would heal the breach.

He strode to the door leading out onto the little balcony. 'Would you be kind enough to show me around the surgery and hospital unit some time before I start work next week?' he asked from the doorway. His voice was cool and professional.

'Of course,' Fee replied. 'Apart from emergencies, I do most visits in the mornings and clinics and surgeries in the afternoons, so early evenings would suit me best, say around sixish. Could you manage that?'

'Certainly. Mrs Shillington—Maggie—says that she is willing to childmind any time, so shall we say the day after tomorrow?'

'Fine,' confirmed Fee, as he turned and made his way down the staircase.

He looked up at her from the bottom, shielding his eyes against the sun. 'Of course, it goes without saying that if I can be of help before I officially start work, I'm ready and willing.'

'Thank you,' said Fee in an icy voice. 'I'll remember that.'

A letter arrived for her in the post before she went back on duty. It was from the health authority, advising her that Dr Cameron had been appointed as resident medical advisor on Drummock as from 10 October. An official meeting would be arranged for her with the doctor in the near future. A handwritten postscript at the bottom of the letter, signed by the Medical Officer of Health, thanked her for all she had done over the last few months.

'So that's that, Fiona McFie,' Fee muttered. 'I hope that you're suitably grateful for those kind words.'

CHAPTER TWO

THE next morning, after her shower, Fee listened to the radio while she dried her hair. The October dawn light was barely brightening the windows. She caught the end of the weather forecast:

A misty morning on the west coast and inner islands, so drive carefully. But when the mist clears, it looks as if it's going to be another hot day. The heat wave isn't over yet, so don't forget the sunscreen, especially for the kiddies. And now to the outer...'

Great, another shorts and loose shirt day. She grinned, remembering how Tom Cameron had stared in surprise at her sleeveless, brief cotton top and had seemed startled that she wasn't in uniform. The grin faded as she brushed her cloud of fine, red-gold hair, already nearly dry and crinkling into soft waves and curls round her face.

Once he was properly in harness, would he try to persuade her to wear a uniform? Well, dream on, Dr Cameron, you haven't a hope. She was her own boss, and the sooner he accepted that, the better. Anyway, what uniform, she thought wryly, to fit which cap— health visitor, midwife, district nurse or general nurse-practitioner? Once dressed, she checked her medical case for the small supply of drugs that she carried with her. She also checked she had syringes, swabs and antiseptic dressings, auriscope, stethoscope and other tools of her various trades.

She had just finished when her mobile rang.

It was six thirty. If the call was professional then it had to be serious for someone to ring so early.

'Good morning. Nurse McFie here. How can I help?' She kept her voice cool and professional to reassure a possibly nervous caller.

'Morning. It's Tom Cameron,' said the doctor briskly. 'I'm at Mrs Cox's house on the corner of Quay Terrace—she does bed and breakfasts.'

Fee stiffened. 'I know who Marie Cox is,' she replied, her voice cooling to freezing. What was *he* doing, phoning her about one of her patients? Why hadn't she been phoned direct? 'She's prone to have falls. What's happened this time?'

'She's had a fall all right—down the stairs. Looks as if the poor soul has a fractured femur. There are all the usual signs—slight discoloured swelling over hip joint, foot averted—and she's in a lot of pain. I've immobilised the leg with makeshift supports—and some pillows—but she needs a shot of morphine, and as I'm not officially on duty until next week, I can't lay my hands on anything stronger than aspirin. What's the drill for obtaining dangerous drugs?'

'I have a small stock and issue them in an emergency. I'll be with you shortly. Meanwhile, phone the air ambulance through the operator. They can get here in twenty minutes or so. I'll call Joe Drummond—he's the part-time ambulance driver. He'll take Marie to the helipad. Joe's not a paramedic, but he's very experienced. He'll have some splints in the ambulance to replace your makeshift ones. I'll be with you with the morphine in a few minutes. Tell Marie that I'm on my way.'

'Will do, Nurse,' he said. His voice was dry, border-ing on sarcastic—or was it just amused? Oh well, at least he'd had the decency to ask for help and hadn't tried to muscle in without putting her in the picture.

She called Joe as she pulled on her shoes, and re-ceived his simple but reassuring 'I'll be there' in reply.

Automatically she picked up her maternity holdall and small oxygen kit as she left her house. There were two almost-mums on the island nearly bursting at the seams. The way things had been going lately it was in the stars that they would both go into labour at the same time. And although the hugely experienced and quite unflap-pable Margot McBain was back from holiday, she *was* beginning to slow down a bit.

'Well, perhaps the handsome Dr Cameron will come in useful after all,' Fee muttered, as she drove down to Marie Cox's B&B. 'I wonder if he's any good on ob-stetrics.'

Less than an hour later, Marie had been safely des-patched to St Catherine's, drowsy and more comfortable, having been given the morphine and with her leg prop-erly immobilised with padded splints.

Marie had been very pleased to see Fee. 'Although,' she had whispered, when the doctor had disappeared for a few minutes and before the morphine Fee had injected had quite taken effect, 'he's a very nice laddie. Just what Drummock needs—a fine, braw-looking doctor.'

Fee had raised her eyes. 'What Drummock needs,' she said through tight lips, 'is a good, competent doctor who knows his stuff.'

'Oh,' Marie had murmured sleepily, 'I thought he did. He…'

She had drifted off then, and Fee had felt mean for

having suggested that the doctor might not be competent when, in fact, they had worked well together and he had proved that he was just that. She couldn't really fault him on procedure.

He had good hands, large with a smattering of fine silvery gold hairs on them. They had been gentle as he and Fee had applied the splints Joe had brought with him. And he had talked to Marie all the time they'd been attending to her, explaining what they were doing even when she'd only just been with it after the injection of morphine.

There was no reason to suppose he was other than a competent doctor and Fee cursed herself for suggesting otherwise. She would put that right, she vowed, when she visited Marie in hospital on the mainland the following day. She herself might not like the man and be suffering humiliation over the matter of his arrival, but that didn't make him a bad doctor.

He had helped Joe load the stretcher into the ambulance and had offered to go with him to the helipad. But Joe had gruffly declined the offer.

'No, thanks, Doctor,' he'd said, formally. 'It's only a few minutes away and the paramedics on the chopper will help me with puir old Marie.' Then he'd turned to Fee pointedly and asked her if there was a note for the hospital.

'Here, just finished it,' Fee had replied, tearing a sheet out of the notebook that she always carried for scribbling basic details down about a patient being admitted as an emergency.

I wonder why Joe doesn't like the new doctor, she thought as the ambulance rumbled away. He was almost rude to him and that's not like Joe.

Her eyes met Tom Cameron's and she blushed.

Should she apologise on Joe's behalf? No, of course not. He hadn't exactly said anything to apologise for. Perhaps the doctor hadn't even noticed.

She turned and went back through the front door with the shining brass knocker.

Tom followed her. 'I rather think,' he said, 'that your Mr Drummond considers me an interloper. Do you think that many islanders will see me in that light?'

Fee shook her head. She hadn't thought about it. 'No, not at all. Most of them will be only too pleased to have you here. Joe just hates change. And he was very fond of the old doctor—'

'And is very fond and protective of you,' interrupted Tom. 'But I wish he had accepted my offer to accompany him, or rather Mrs Cox, to the helipad. I'm not very happy about her going off unescorted.'

He's not very happy, thought Fee. Well, tough. This was what she'd been dreading—a doctor coming to the island who hadn't a clue about Drummock and its unique needs and its own way of doing things. A doctor who just couldn't wait to impose his own ideas.

Almost biting her lip in an effort not to say the wrong thing, she took a deep breath.

'Well, there are often occasions when the two of us have to work on our own. And unless I can free one of my nurses to go as escort, and they are frequently stretched to the limit, or get a neighbour to go along, Joe has to take a patient on his own. And, of course, there isn't really any risk. Nowhere is very far away on the island, whether it's our own little medical unit or the helipad.'

He frowned. 'Point taken. But in this case I was available and could have gone along.'

'Yes, and it was good of you to offer.' She could think

of no excuse for Joe's rejection so she added ruefully, 'I'm afraid that Joe is rather set in his ways.'

Even saying as little as that made her feel a traitor to the hard-working ambulance driver, who was also, like so many of the islanders, a voluntary lifeguard. This was what visitors couldn't understand. A place like Drummock couldn't function without a lot of give and take. Sometimes rules had to be bent, if not broken.

But it was also true that many of the residents, especially the older inhabitants, were wary of strangers. Dr Cameron would be welcomed on the whole because, in spite of all that Fee herself could do, having a resident doctor would save a lot of hassle.

Certain cases which at present had to be shipped to the mainland might be able to be cared for in their own little five-bedded hospital unit. But only, she thought darkly, glancing quickly at Dr Cameron, if he was willing to learn and accept them as they were.

The doctor was looking thoughtful. After a moment, he said, 'Well, I'll try not to step on Joe's or anyone else's toes. But I have certain standards and won't be able to turn a blind eye all the time.'

'No one would expect you to,' replied Fee. 'You have to do what your conscience demands. I just ask you to bear these things in mind.'

Marie's house was empty now. Joe wouldn't return once he'd seen Marie on board the helicopter. And the B&B guest who had alerted the doctor of Marie's fall had gone on his way, warmed by Fee's thanks for acting so promptly in getting assistance and delighted to have been recompensed by a free night's lodging.

Tom frowned at Fee. 'Bit high-handed weren't you? Didn't you go too far, waiving that chap's payment for the night without Mrs Cox's approval? It was a generous gesture, but after all the B&B is her living.'

'It's what Marie would have done to show her gratitude, had she had her wits about her.'

'How can you be so sure?'

Fee shrugged. 'It's the way we are on Drummock. We don't like being beholden to anyone, and I guess we just like giving. Charity appeals go well here, whether they're national ones or local events. We may be a tiny island, Dr Cameron, but we can hold our own and pay our way.'

His deep blue eyes were unreadable but he raised his eyebrows and his wide mouth curled sardonically at one side.

'Is that why you resent my presence, Nurse McFie, because you're hell bent on holding your own? I guess you don't want me intruding on your territory, which has been your sole responsibility for months. I can understand that.'

In the process of packing up her case, Fee paused. Was there a grain of truth in what he was saying? No, there couldn't be! She had been looking forward to having a resident doctor on the island to share her workload. At least, she thought, trying to be honest, I did in the beginning. But now...

She stared at him, and the uncertainty must have shown in her eyes.

He said coolly, 'I'm right, aren't I? You've got used to managing everything yourself, making decisions about the best course of treatment for a patient, ordering tests and so on, as well as doing the more mundane tasks. I don't blame you for wanting to hang onto that power.'

'You make me sound power crazy,' said Fee, as a

wave of anger washed over her. 'But someone had to do it when the old doctor went, and I have never stepped outside the brief that I'm trained for. I worked hard for all my qualifications from the time I was seventeen and a half till I was twenty-five.'

'And now you've had a chance to put them all into action,' stated Tom. 'That's how I felt when I first qualified sixteen years ago. I was twenty-two and things were not quite so cynical then as they are now. There was still some respect around for doctors. And suddenly I was the person who was supposed to know all the answers. *You* know yourself that you don't have all the answers, but it's a hell of a morale-booster to inspire that sort of faith in others, though it can be frightening, too.'

'Why are you telling me all this, Dr Cameron?' asked Fee, putting the last of her bits and pieces away in her case.

'Because I want you to know that I understand how you feel about suddenly finding…' He didn't finish the sentence, but frowned and pushed back a swathe of flaxen hair, a puzzled expression on his handsome, boyish face.

'That I've had a new and unannounced doctor who knows nothing about Drummock, or the people who live here, dumped upon me?' Fee said. 'A man that some of the medics on the mainland will be happy to deal with in a way that they were reluctant to deal with me. A man who wants to play boss—'

'Who said anything about wanting to play boss?' Tom interrupted, looking grim.

'You don't have to say it,' replied Fee drily. 'Even in shorts and sandals, you look the part. And there are plenty of people around who will automatically assume that you are the boss, simply because you're a man.'

'Ah, sexism rears its ugly head even on this beautiful island.'

'You'd better believe it,' said Fee. 'It was a struggle in the beginning to get people to accept me as a substitute doctor, even though I had virtually been doing the job as our old doctor got frailer. I was respected, trusted as Fee McFie, nurse and midwife, but now…' She shrugged hopelessly.

'And now, just as you're beginning to make it work, a big bad new doctor comes along and you're back to square one.'

'Something like that,' she answered. 'Oh, well, that's the way the cookie crumbles. I'll survive. Anyway, it's not your problem. With a few exceptions you'll be welcomed with open arms.'

In some strange sort of way, she wished that he wasn't being so understanding about it. For some reason it made his presence harder to bear.

She snapped her case shut and picked it up. 'Well, I must get cracking. I've two babies fighting to get out into the big wide world any moment now, and I bet they arrive within hours of each other.'

He said tentatively, 'Are they both home deliveries? Because if they are and you want a hand, just ask.'

'Thanks, but Margot McBain and I can manage.'

'Oh.' He sounded disappointed. 'Who is Margot McBain?'

'A semi-retired midwife who helps out when necessary. She's an absolute gem. Now, I must ask you to go, Dr Cameron. I've got to lock up and leave a message on the answering machine to let people know that Marie won't be taking any B&B guests for the time being.'

The doctor moved toward the door and looked at his watch.

'Good Lord, I hadn't realised the time. I'd better go home and feed my kids, if they haven't already started themselves, in which case the kitchen will be knee deep in cornflakes.' He smiled an affectionate, tolerant smile, as any loving father would have.

Fee felt a little tug of guilt. She hadn't given a thought to his children—or the fact that he'd had to leave them. Though Quay House was only a few hundred yards away, it couldn't have been easy, leaving them on their first morning on Drummock.

She walked with him along the passage to the front door. 'Thanks for coming to Marie's rescue,' she said. 'I'm sorry that you had to leave your children. But Drummock's a very safe place for youngsters, and I'm sure that Maggie Shillington will always stand in if you need her.'

'"A very safe place",' he repeated softly. 'I like the sound of that...' Then a shadow passed across his face, wiping out the boyish expression. 'That's what I want for my kids—a safe place.' He raised a hand in farewell, and walked away down the quay.

I wonder what sort of secret he's hiding, mused Fee as she closed up the B&B. Something's bugging him, but what?

Her mobile went as she was letting herself out of the front door.

'Hello, there, Fee,' said Ian McKay, in his soft island accent. 'I got back last night—and just in time it seems. Shelagh's waters have broken. You know her—that means that she's going to drop the baby any minute now.'

Fee grinned to herself and said sharply, 'Ian, we're not talking about one of your precious cows calving, but your wife giving birth. I'll be there in ten minutes.'

She arrived at the farm just in time to steer the baby out between Shelagh's legs. 'It's a girl, Shelagh,' she said joyfully, knowing that both she and Ian had wanted a girl to make up the perfect set of two girls and two boys. And she's lovely.'

She laid the babe across Shelagh's suddenly slack abdomen and waited for the afterbirth to descend, whilst Shelagh cooed at and cuddled the slippery little creature. The sight of a new mum bonding with her infant never ever failed to move Fee almost to tears, in spite of the hundreds of babies she'd delivered.

Ian, who had been hovering around anxiously, put out a large, horny hand and stroked the baby's wet head with his forefinger, then he bent and kissed her and his wife.

'I'll tell the kids and your mum, and make us a cuppa—with a splash of my special malt in it,' he said, disappearing through the door.

'Make mine and Shelagh's a very small splash,' Fee said, wondering as she said it what Dr Cameron would think of the centuries-old island custom of tea and whisky after the birth of a baby.

Was this one of the things he would have a conscience about, draw the line at? If he did, he was in for big trouble.

Fortified by the strong tea laced with whisky, Fee, with help from Shelagh's mum who had come to look after Ian and the children for a week or so, washed and tidied up the new mother and baby, and made up the bed with clean sheets.

'I'll be back this evening to see you, Shelagh,' Fee promised. 'Make the most of your mum being here and take it easy.'

She made a couple of visits on her way back to her flat, one in her role as district nurse to an elderly lady with a slow-healing varicose ulcer. Her other, wearing her locum hat, was to make a diagnosis on a middle-aged man who was breathless and wheezing with what sounded like bronchitis, to which he was prone.

Both patients wanted to know about the new doctor. What did Fee think of him? When was he going to start work? Was it true that his wife had left him with two puir little bairns to look after? And was he a big braw man with long, nearly white hair, rather wild-looking?

Fee re-dressed the ulcer with a new cream that was supposed to work wonders, and answered as best she could, or thought appropriate.

On her second visit, Rob could hardly wait for her to listen to his chest with her stethoscope before bombarding her with similar questions.

She continued resolutely with her duty first. 'It sounds like a rugger match going on in there,' she said, tapping his chest. 'I'll write you up for your usual antibiotics— that should put you right in a week or so.'

'But what do you think, Fee?' Rob persisted. 'Is this new man going to be a help to you, or is he going to put your nose out of joint?'

'We'll be colleagues,' said Fee evenly. 'We'll work together, just like the old doctor and I used to work.'

'Oh, aye,' replied Rob laconically, his voice full of doubt. 'I can't see it working out. You've been the boss for a long time Fee, even before the old doctor retired. Some of us could see that. You won't want to knuckle under to a new broom who wants to change everything, will you?'

It was difficult to avoid the direct question and it surprised her to hear how much her situation was being considered. It was flattering to learn that so many people

cared for her, but a little daunting, too. Drummock people could be fiercely protective of their own and at the
same time freeze out strangers. It mustn't, Fee realised,
be allowed to get out of hand. It spelt trouble. It could
divide the island if some people supported her and some
the new doctor.

'It won't come to that,' she said firmly. 'Dr Cameron
will want to make things work as well as I do.'

'If you say so,' said Rob, clearly not believing a word
of it.

'But don't worry, lass, you'll have plenty of support.'

Fee drove away from Rob's house feeling shattered.

Even knowing the effectiveness of the local grape-
vine, she was amazed at the speed with which the news
had travelled. Much of it was because Tom Cameron
had arrived unannounced, had two children but no wife
in evidence, and apparently possessed a mysterious history. If some of the islanders were already thinking the
way that Rob was, the future between herself and the
doctor looked bumpy to say the least.

For her own part, she was ready to grit her teeth and
go along with him as much as possible, and if necessary
act as mediator between him and the patients. But there
was one area of the practice that she felt strongly
about—home deliveries. That traditionally was the midwives' province, and would remain that way unless his
medical expertise was needed in an emergency.

There were plenty of home births on the island, since
people born and bred on Drummock liked to have their
babies on the spot and be proud of the title, a 'Drum
baby'. She and Margot had always attended to these,
calling in the doctor only if there was a problem that
was beyond their expertise. They also ran good antenatal

classes and generally picked up any difficulties that might arise and dealt with them in good time.

Only if a patient requested an epidural or experienced any serious complications was she hospitalised on the mainland. But this was always a last resort and Fee hoped that the doctor would respect the desire of most women to have their babies on Drummock.

This was something she would have to discuss with him in the near future, perhaps tomorrow when they did their tour of the medical unit and surgery. He would have to be put in the picture about all manner of things pertaining to his role as medical officer.

She had no idea what he had been told by the officials on the mainland—not a lot, she imagined, since it had been three weeks since a doctor had visited Drummock and held a surgery.

And for a long time the buck has stopped with me, Fee thought as she wallowed in a cooling, scented bath that night. But now it would stop at Dr Thomas Cameron's large chest. The health of the islanders was no longer her prime responsibility but his.

She got out of the bath and towelled herself vigorously.

'Well, Fiona McFie,' she murmured to her blurred image in the steamy mirror, 'the nurses are still your direct responsibility. It'll be up to you to see that they keep up to scratch.'

She went to sleep and dreamed of fighting a duel with Tom Cameron. Unfortunately, she woke up before the contest was concluded.

Oh, well, that's life, she thought, full of unfinished business. And only then did she realise that in the excitement of delivering the baby she hadn't even mentioned the new doctor's unexpected arrival to Ian. Well, no doubt he'd hear of it soon enough. By tomorrow she doubted if there'd be anyone on the island who wouldn't know about it.

CHAPTER THREE

FEE'S first call next day came from Margot McBain.

'Fee, I think you should come. I'm with Blanche Forrester. James called me as I'm so near. She's just started labour and the baby's turned suddenly and is lying in a transverse position. Blanche didn't want to call us earlier as everything appeared to be going along fine.'

'That's Blanche all over, isn't it? Not wanting to be a nuisance,' said Fee. 'I'll be with you shortly.'

Fee quickly collected Blanche's notes from the surgery, although she knew her history off by heart and didn't really need them. A transverse position would be difficult to manage, she thought, especially as labour had just started.

This was Blanche's third baby. She had attended all her antenatal classes, and when Fee had seen her last week everything had been on track for an uncomplicated delivery. The only thing that puzzled Fee slightly was that she had expected both Blanche's baby and Shelagh's to put in an appearance on the same day and her instincts rarely let her down. Had the twenty-hour delay made any difference?

She wished now that she had obeyed those instincts and gone to check up on Blanche after delivering Shelagh's baby the day before. But she had still been rattled by the arrival of the new doctor, one of the rare occasions when she had let personal feelings intrude on the professional. She comforted herself with the thought that even if she had checked on Blanche, according to

Margot she would have found everything in order as the baby had only just decided to turn itself. But that didn't alter the fact that she should have popped in yesterday to see that all was well.

If it hadn't been for that wretched man…

Well, it wouldn't happen again, she told herself. Concentrate on what you're doing when you get to Blanche, McFie. Would there be time to turn the baby? She had done it several times in the earlier stages of pregnancy but only once after labour had started, and it wasn't easy.

As the weather forecaster had said, there was still heavy mist about, especially on the coastal road, and she had to crawl along. It took her twenty minutes to reach Blanche's house when it should have taken ten.

She was met by James, Blanche's husband, usually a calm, unexcitable man as befitted the manager of the little local bank. He was, for once, looking decidedly agitated.

'Thank God you've come,' he said. 'Nurse McBain is doing what she can, but Blanche is in a lot of pain. Nurse wanted to give her an injection, but she refused. Said that she wanted it to be natural, as the others had been.' He laid a hand on Fee's arm as she climbed out of the Land Rover. 'Look, Fee, if there's any question between Blanche and the baby…' His voice trailed away.

Fee said gently but cheerfully, 'Don't even think like that, James. The baby's not in the best of positions, but Margot and I have handled similar situations before. Now, come up and hold your wife's hand. That's what she needs—only don't faint on me.'

James followed her upstairs, looking somewhat reassured.

Blanche was half kneeling, half crouching beside the bed, her face buried in her arms.

Fee had a quick, whispered conversation with Margot, and then knelt down beside Blanche.

'Blanche, I need to give you an internal examination,' she said softly, 'and it's not possible whilst you're kneeling down like this. Would you get back on the bed for a few minutes, please?'

James said, 'Come on sweetheart, I'll help you up.'

With a faint moan, which she tried to muffle, Blanche crawled up onto the bed.

Margot handed Fee a pair of latex gloves, which she pulled on before carefully beginning her examination. She straightened up after a few moments and nodded at Margot.

'Yep. As you say, a transverse lie.' To Blanche and James, she said, 'The baby is lying across the uterus—the womb. I'm going to try to turn it into the right position with the head down where it should be when it's entering the birth canal. But, Blanche, for me to do that I need to give you an injection to relax you and ease the pain, which will be considerable. I know that you want a natural birth, but if you want to keep the baby safe, it's a necessity. You wouldn't object to having an anaesthetic if you were going to have an operation, so think of this as a minor op.'

They all held their breaths, and the silence was broken only by Blanche's noisy breathing.

'All right,' she murmured at last through a moan of pain. 'If it's best for the baby.'

Fee gave her a shot of pethidine mixed with a muscle relaxant, and pulled on sterile gloves while she waited for it to work.

It took a while to manoeuvre the baby back into the normal cephalic presentation, and her fingers and wrists ached with the effort. Blanche was wonderful at controlling the contractions that were slowly building up, so that Fee could get on with the job of turning the foetus around.

Thank goodness labour hadn't been too advanced when the baby had swivelled into the transverse position, or she couldn't have done anything. That would have meant that the baby might have been delivered with a shoulder or elbow coming out first, very painful for the mother and possibly be life-threatening for the baby if the process took too long.

Margot monitored the baby's heartbeat as Fee worked. She nodded from time to time that all was well. Eventually, Fee turned the baby into the right position, head downwards, ready to start its journey into the world. She took off her gloves with a sigh of relief and rubbed her aching wrists.

Again Margot recorded the baby's heartbeat and confirmed that all was well. 'A little fast, but as steady as a rock,' she told Fee. She gave James, who, white-faced, was clutching his wife's hand, the thumbs-up sign. 'You've got a little toughie in there,' she said.

James nodded. 'But what about my Blanche?' he asked, bending to kiss his wife's pale, sweaty cheek. 'Is she all right? That's the main thing.'

Blanche, still half knocked out by the injection, murmured, 'I'm all right, love. Is the baby OK?'

Fee answered her. 'Baby's fine,' she said, 'and has come through with flying colours, though you've a long way to go yet. Labour's only just started, but now that the little one is back in position we should begin to make progress. Margot is going to take your blood pressure, temperature and pulse, and tidy you up a bit, and James and I are going downstairs to make a cup of tea.'

'Oh,' said James uncertainly. 'Are we?'

'Yes,' replied Fee, nudging him out of the room.

Once in the kitchen, she pushed him into a chair and said, 'I'll make the tea. You look as if you could do with a cup.'

She busied herself with the kettle and mugs.

James said in a surprised voice, 'How do you know where everything is?'

'Because I've made tea here before, when I've visited the children when they've been ill and when I delivered your last little one.' She grinned. 'I know where to find things in most people's houses.'

'You're such a busy woman.' James's voice was full of admiration. His colour was returning as the worst of his shock over Blanche abated. 'Drummock couldn't manage without you.' Then he added rather uncertainly, 'Is it true that we've suddenly acquired a doctor on the island?'

'Yes, although he doesn't start working officially until next week. But I'm glad that you've mentioned it. I'd like to ask him to look at Blanche. Turning the baby wasn't easy at this stage and she's taken quite a pummelling. I could ask a doctor to come over from the mainland, but it seems daft to do that when we've someone on the spot. Anyway, if someone came over they'd probably want to take her back for the delivery.'

James, a great stickler for tradition, clenched his hands and shook his head. 'They couldn't do that! We've had both the children on Drummock and we were both born on Drummock. I thought you said that Blanche was all right and fit to go on with labour,' he added, sounding slightly belligerent.

'She is. I just want to get a second opinion from a doctor. As I explained, doing that procedure when labour has started is a bit tricky. Her pelvic muscles are bruised.

He may be able to suggest how we can best help make the rest of her labour easier.'

'But if he hasn't started work yet, how do you know that he's any good. What are his credentials?'

'Oh, he's good. I worked with him yesterday when Mrs Cox broke her leg. And his credentials are excellent,' confirmed Fee, crossing her fingers.

Well, he *had* been great with Marie, she admitted to herself. And the expression on his face when she'd said she was going to do a delivery had said a lot. She might not like the man, might have to go into battle with him if he started meddling in their customs, but right now she needed that second opinion, and he was on the doorstep.

She pushed a mug over to James. 'So, shall I call him?'

James nodded. 'If you think it's best.'

It was, thought Fee, one of the hardest phone calls she'd had to make, at least on a personal level. She was going to ask the man who had offered his services, and whom she had turned down, to do her a favour and offer an opinion on *her* patient—well, hers and Margot's. The man whom she still didn't want here on the island.

'But it's for the patient's welfare, so I must,' she murmured, as she went outside to make the call on her mobile, leaving James to take tea up to Margot and his wife.

One part of her rather hoped that someone else would answer and say that the doctor was out. After all, he was on holiday and had his children to entertain. But another part of her realised that that wouldn't be a good option. If he wasn't willing to do the job, she would have to get someone from the mainland, and the first thing that they would want to do would be to transfer Blanche to St Cath's.

Of course, Dr Cameron might want to do the same. He might not want to stick his neck out and make a professional call before he was officially employed by the health authorities, although he'd offered to do so.

This was exactly what he said when he answered the phone and heard her request. 'I'm not quite sure how I stand,' he said. 'It was different with Mrs Cox—that was an emergency. But this isn't exactly, although I agree with you that the lady should be looked at.'

There was a pause, and Fee's heart plummeted.

Then he said, 'Look, leave it with me. I've got an idea. I'll get back to you as soon as I can.' He put down the phone before she could reply.

What sort of a solution could he find in a short time? Damn the man, he was shrouded in mystery. A sense of fair play told her that she couldn't really blame him. It was the fault and discourtesy of the admin people who had allowed this to happen. Hopefully, all or part would be revealed when they started working together next week. Surely then he would open up and tell her something of his personal history.

He was quite right, of course. The situation with Marie had been very different and the help she was looking for now was much more subtle. It was the sort of situation which any doctor might find him- or herself in and seek a second opinion. If he was speaking to someone on the mainland to get permission to offer that second opinion, she hoped that he would find one of the medical people to talk to who would understand the problem.

With all her heart, she wished that she hadn't had to ask for his help. In the months she'd acted as locum, she'd only had to ask for assistance a few times. Yet this man had only been on Drummock a couple of days, and twice she'd found herself indebted to him…

Her mobile buzzed and she snatched it out of her pocket.

'Well, as from now, I am the officially appointed medical officer to Drummock,' Tom said. 'Now, tell me, where do I have to go?'

She gave him directions to Rowan Point and the Forresters' house.

She briefed him when he arrived some fifteen minutes later, filling him in on Blanche's previous two trouble-free deliveries and the so-far smooth running of this pregnancy.

'The baby turned without warning,' she explained, 'but because the contractions were still weak and far apart, I decided that there was still time to correct it.'

'I'd have done the same,' Tom said. 'Any doctor would if there was a chance of a normal delivery.'

He sounded sincere and reassuring.

Fee put a hand on his arm. 'Before we go up, can I, please, explain that it is very important to islanders that their babies are born on Drummock.' She dropped her hand from his bronzed arm. 'I hope that you won't find it necessary to transfer Blanche to St Cath's.'

Tom looked down at where her hand had rested. 'I don't see why it should be,' he said, 'with a good team here to look after her.'

They went upstairs and Fee introduced him to Blanche, James and Margot.

He sat on the side of the bed, smiled at Blanche and looked at the chart Margot handed him containing the latest figures on blood pressure, temperature and pulse, and the timing of contractions.

'You're doing fine,' he said. He took Blanche's hand and his fingers found her radial pulse. 'That's good,' he added after a moment. 'Now, I'd like to have a look at your tummy. I think you'll have a few bruises after the pummelling Nurse McFie has given you, but that can't be helped. And then I'll do an internal examination to confirm that everything's going along as it should be.'

He was marvellous. He put Blanche and everyone at their ease.

Fee watched him with mixed feelings, reminding herself frequently that this was what she'd wanted, what Drummock needed and deserved—a caring doctor. But would it last? He looked as if he might have come from a smart city practice, either in Britain or abroad, used to taking long holidays in the sun. How would someone like that fit into island life?

At the moment it was fine and beautiful on the island. But in winter the weather coming in off the Atlantic was often treacherous. Gales blew from west to east across the island, trailing the shreds of huge hurricanes from North America. And sometimes Drummock was cut off from the mainland. Occasionally they lost their electricity and had to rely on other forms of lighting and heating.

How would he manage then, even though Maggie Shillington would be in her element and make herself available at all times, with two children to care for?

His voice cut across her musings and she thought, as she had when they'd first met, what a pleasant voice it was.

He was speaking to Blanche. 'Everything's fine. The baby is just where it should be. But your tummy is very bruised, and you will feel the stretch in all your muscles when your contractions get stronger, but that's only to be expected. Don't be afraid to have some gas and air. Don't try to be heroic.'

Blanche pulled a face. 'I so wanted this one to be like the other two.'

'I know.' Tom's voice was gentle and sympathetic. 'Nurse Fee told me that you wanted a natural birth, and I respect that, and it would be fine if everything had remained straightforward. But you have to accept that it hasn't been. Manipulation of a foetus at any time is difficult, and rarely done once labour has started. But Nurse did the right thing in trying, and she was successful. Don't spoil her efforts by refusing any help you can get.'

'Of course, you're right,' said Blanche. 'It wouldn't be fair, too selfish…' She winced and drew up her legs as a contraction hit her.

They all waited until the contraction had passed, with James gripping her hands and looking as pained as she was.

Tom broke the silence first.

'About this bruising of your abdomen,' he said. 'The bruising of your deeper muscles will only respond to painkillers, which we will give when necessary. But I expect Nurse Fee or Nurse McBain will think of something that will help keep your superficial muscles as supple as possible. One old patient I had used to swear by witch hazel to soothe bruises.'

Margot McBain, who had eyed him rather suspiciously when Fee had introduced him, now beamed at him. 'That was my granny's recipe,' she said. 'Mixed with a little lavender oil. I'd clean forgotten about it.' She squeezed Blanche's shoulder gently. 'We'll try that, I've got both at home.'

The doctor smiled at James. 'I think we men are *de trop*,' he said. 'Shall we leave the ladies to it? I noticed that you have some magnificent late hollyhocks in your garden. May I take a closer look at them?'

It was masterly, thought Fee, the way he steered James out of the bedroom. Over his shoulder, he said, 'If I may have a word before I go, Nurse?'

Fee joined the two men in the garden ten minutes later. James looked quite animated and relaxed as he pointed out various plants in the herbaceous border.

With a mental shrug, Fee acknowledged that Tom Cameron appeared to have won over another Drummock resident. First there'd been Maggie Shillington, who had taken him and his 'puir wee bairns' under her wing within hours of him arriving on Drummock. Then Marie Cox, who'd thought him 'a braw lad' when he'd tended her broken leg.

And only a few minutes ago she'd left Blanche and Margot singing his praises. Now here was James, who only shortly before had been expressing his doubts about the man, obviously enjoying the doctor's company.

Not surprising. The doctor had succeeded in reassuring him that his wife was doing well, which, considering his temperament, was quite an achievement on short acquaintance. The others had found him reassuring, too, but, then, he was that sort of man. It was what patients needed— reassurance.

But Fee was rather surprised, and a little…*hurt*? It was ridiculous, she told herself, that Margot, old stalwart that she was, seemed to have been bowled over so completely. Margot didn't have a particularly high opinion of most doctors, having worked with dozens over the years, which was one of the reasons she had returned to Drummock to work exclusively in midwifery. Yet in minutes Tom Cameron had charmed her as he appeared to charm everyone else.

Well, it's no good beefing about it, mused Fee as she approached the two men. Just as long as he didn't decide that island life wasn't for him and take off as suddenly as he'd arrived.

She smiled at James. 'Blanche is all tidied up and looking much more her usual happy self,' she said, 'but would like you there to hold her hand.'

James shook Tom's hand. 'Goodbye, Doctor, and thank you.'

'All thanks are to Nurse Fee,' Tom said. 'She did all the hard work. I just came in to admire her handiwork.' His smile embraced both James and Fee.

I wish he hadn't said that, thought Fee, as if he meant it.

'Oh, Fee's brilliant,' said James, as he strode away toward the house. 'The best.'

'How's our lady doing?' asked Tom, suddenly very professional.

'Her contractions have speeded up slightly and we've put her on two-hourly obs. Margot, who only lives a few doors along, will pop in and out to do those, and she'll contact me if there's any need.'

'Would it be in order if she contacted me as well,' he asked, 'if anything out of the way crops up, or when delivery is imminent? I won't get in the way. She's your case. I'd just like to be there. It's been a while since...' He shrugged his broad shoulders.

Fee didn't really want him to be there, even as an onlooker, but she could hardly refuse after what he'd done. She tried to instil some warmth into her voice.

'Of course,' she replied, 'but, as I'm sure you know, it might be late before she delivers. What about your children? You wouldn't want to leave them alone at night, would you?'

He shook his head and grinned. 'Not even on safe

Drummock,' he said. 'Maggie Shillington's coming in to stay the night.'

Fee's lips tightened. 'So you'd already decided to be in at the birth,' she said accusingly. 'I don't know why you bothered to ask!'

Leaving him gaping, she turned on her heel and stalked back to the house.

This was what she'd feared. That he would take it for granted that, as the island's doctor, he had a right to show up where and when he wanted. He might look like every woman's ideal knight in shining armour, with his golden tan and blond hair, but all he represented to Fee was the man with whom she was going to have to do battle, day in and day out. He would throw his considerable weight about and let her and everyone know who was boss.

No way could she see him being prepared to play the role of partner. One look at that aristocratic nose made it plain that he would be determined to be in charge. Her first impression, that he was easygoing and laid back, had vanished. He was like so many men—full of himself and his importance. She was surprised that Margot hadn't seen through him.

She breathed in deeply as she went into the house. Well, they would have to work together eventually, but not before she had made a few ground rules. One more look at Blanche and then she would be on her way, doing her usual rounds.

What a relief it would be to get on with her daily chores and forget Tom Cameron for the time being. Pretend that he didn't exist, that his coming had been a bad dream.

*   *   *

An angry phone call from Ian McKay when she got home for lunch scrubbed that idea. He had just found a letter from the authorities on the mainland informing him of the appointment of Dr Cameron, 'subject to his approval' which, in fact, they had presumed, he told Fee. 'Why on earth didn't you tell me about him, Fee?'

Fee laughed. 'What, when you arrived home and found Shelagh in labour? Or when you were in the middle of enjoying the safe arrival of your new baby?'

'Fair enough. Point taken. So what's this chap like? will he fit in, do you think? Or will he throw his weight about and try to take over from you? If he does, he'll have a war on his hands. I'm glad that you're getting help, Fee, you deserve it, but not at the expense of losing your authority.'

'Oh, well, only time will tell,' replied Fee philosophically, but a little frisson of wariness trickled through her at the thought of two factions dividing the island.

CHAPTER FOUR

FEE calmed down a little as she made her rounds.

She would have to try to be civil to Tom. She'd made her point and now perhaps she should offer a small olive branch. She was due to hold a surgery at the hospital that afternoon and it occurred to her that now Tom Cameron was officially appointed Medical Officer he might want to take it. It was, after all, a doctor's surgery, though only occasionally in the last few months had a doctor been in attendance. If he wanted to do it, so be it.

She tried to approach the idea in a casual fashion, as if it didn't matter—though, of course, it did. It would be very, very hard to give up the locum part of her working day, though she would soon fill it with other calls on her time. How often, she reminded herself, had she worked until late evening to get all her jobs done? And she hadn't taken a full day off in ages.

Well, in future she might be able to get home at a reasonable time each day, perhaps to see some of these programmes on TV that she was always missing and, whilst the evenings were still light enough, do a bit of gardening and put in some plants for the autumn and winter.

Decisively, she drew up off the road and rang Tom on her mobile.

But the telephone at Quay House, after ringing for a bit, merely spilled out a recorded message in the doctor's voice. 'Dr Cameron is not available at the moment.

Please leave your name and number and he'll ring you back as soon as possible. In an emergency, ring Nurse McFie on…' Her number followed.

'He's gone off without as much as a by your leave,' Fee fumed. Should she leave a message? Was he the doctor here, or wasn't he? The fact that the old doctor would have done the same cut no ice with her in her present mood. No, why should she leave a message? She had tried to contact him and if he now missed the surgery it was too bad.

Her cheeks reddened and she tightened her fingers on the steering wheel and drove off again. 'Don't be so childish, McFie,' she muttered. 'Try phoning him again when you get home.'

She didn't have to. The phone was ringing as she entered the flat. It was Tom Cameron.

He said without preamble, 'Can you get over to The Crow's Nest and bring Captain Mackintosh's notes? He's had a stroke, a massive one. I need to know what medication he's on and something of his current and previous history. His housekeeper—' he lowered his voice '—if I understand her correctly, reckons that you're the only person who will know what to do. In fact, I believe she meant to phone you and dialled Quay House by mistake.'

An extraordinary mixture of emotions washed over Fee. Sorrow that the old captain had had a stroke, although it had been more or less inevitable, yet amusement that the doctor couldn't understand Mrs Mack— no relation to the captain. Few people could as she spoke in a very soft Highland dialect. Lastly Fee felt a warm, slightly smug feeling that she was needed.

Her thoughts were fleeting and she answered him quickly enough.

'It'll take me twenty-five minutes to get there, stopping off at the surgery for his notes on the way. It's the furthest point on the island. Do you want me to bring anything else?'

There was a moment's hesitation, then he said, 'Your usual bag of tricks will be enough, I think, but some oxygen might be useful. God, I'll be glad when I get my case stocked up.'

'I can imagine,' Fee replied drily, adding to herself, You're doing pretty well building up a practice without any gear.

To Fee's delight, the rather austere old housekeeper was really pleased to see her, and gabbled away in her soft dialect the minute that Fee stepped through the door into the large entrance hall of the house built around the base of the lighthouse itself.

Captain Mackintosh was lying at the foot of the narrow winding staircase leading up to the glassed-in roof area that gave the house its name. It had once been a lighthouse and was perfect for the old captain, whose hobby was astronomy—or 'star gazing' as he called it. A ready-made observatory.

Tom was crouching beside the prone figure, shining a pen-light into the captain's eyes.

Fee crossed from the door and knelt beside the old man as Tom tested his reflexes. The reflexes were jerky and over-brisk, a typical reaction with a stroke victim.

There was nothing boyish about the doctor's face now. His dark blond eyebrows were drawn into a frown above his aristocratic nose as he concentrated hard. A thick lock of flaxen hair fell across his forehead. To her dismay, Fee found herself wanting to push it back into place.

He nodded to Fee, and said brusquely, 'Will you ask Mrs Mack if he fell down the stairs, or was at the bottom when she found him? It would be useful to know how he fell. As far as I can see, there are no injuries consistent with falling down the stairs. She's not related to him, is she?'

'No. Half the islanders are Mac-something.'

'I see. Meanwhile, may I beg a loan of your stethoscope and sphygmo, and an airway. Then I can make a rather better job of examining the poor chap. The few medical bits and pieces that I still possess are buried somewhere in my main luggage, which only came off the ferry this morning.'

Medical equipment that he still possessed? What on earth did he mean by that? Doctors looked after their instruments. They were expensive items.

'I'll do what I can,' Fee said, keeping her voice low and even, 'but I don't always understand Mrs Mack either.' She opened her surgical case and took out her stethoscope, a neat electronic blood pressure kit and an airway, and handed them to him.

'Thanks.' He ran the stethoscope over the captain's chest. 'Heart's sluggish, only working at half-cock,' he said. 'And lungs congested, just as one would expect.' He was half talking to himself. He took the patient's blood pressure and frowned.

Fee turned to the housekeeper. 'Mrs Mack, do you know if the captain fell downstairs, or was he near the bottom when he fell?'

Mrs Mack shook her head. In her almost incomprehensible accent she said, 'Nae, the puir wee man.' Fee hid a smile. The captain was six feet-something and broad. 'He just collapsed all of a heap as he put his foot on the first step. I couldna get to him in time to stop him falling.'

Just as well, thought Fee, he would have squashed her.

Mrs Mack peered into Fee's face and added solemnly, 'It was nae a surprise to me, lass. He hasna been too bonny for a wee while, wheezing like a kettle on the hob.'

'That's useful to know about his chest,' said the doctor, giving Mrs Mack a quick smile of thanks.

Mrs Mack nodded as if that were obvious. 'I'm away now,' she said, 'to get more blankets to cover the captain with. The puir man might as well be made as snug as nature allows.'

'Well,' Tom said when the housekeeper had disappeared through a doorway, 'I caught the bit about the wheezy chest. Good description that, kettle on the hob. But did he fall?'

'No,' Fee replied. 'Apparently he collapsed at the first step. From what Mrs Mack says, he hasn't been well for a while and she wasn't surprised to see him collapse.'

'Why on earth didn't he call you in? You might have foreseen this. Or is he one of the old brigade who don't like women medics or are shy of them?'

Fee grinned. 'Shy of women? Not the captain. If he's to be believed, he literally did have a girl in every port in the world, as all good sailors should have. When he's well, he still has a definite twinkle in his eye.'

Just for a moment they were on the same wavelength, and smiled at each other. 'The old sea dog,' murmured Tom admiringly.

Then, just as suddenly, they stopped smiling and looked embarrassed, as if they'd been caught doing something wrong.

'But I wonder why he didn't ask me to call,' mused

Fee, looking down at the captain to avoid Tom's eyes. 'He knows that I'm only too happy to come.'

Tom finished his examination, and she handed him the captain's medical notes.

'As you see, he's not on much medication. A diuretic which he takes occasionally. Enough to keep his fluid balance under control. He was on Adalat Retard for his hypertension, but he often didn't take it. Said it made him feel worse. After conferring with a medic on the mainland, I stopped supplying it. There didn't seem any point.'

'The point is,' said Tom flatly, 'that this might not have happened had his blood pressure been treated.'

Fee stared at him, and then asked in a colourless voice, 'Are you saying, Doctor, that it's my fault the captain has had a stroke?'

'No, Nurse. I'm saying that it might have been worth pressing him to take the medication, or seeking out some alternative that did suit him.'

That was precisely what Fee had suggested to Dr Forster when she'd phoned for advice. But Forster had argued that if the captain didn't want medication it shouldn't be forced on him. There was some truth in that, of course, but she'd had a suspicion that this was an economy rather than an opportunity to give the patient a choice.

Taking several deep breaths in an effort to regain her cool, Fee debated with herself whether to tell Tom Cameron that. No, she decided, it would sound as if she were making excuses. Let him think what he liked, his opinion didn't bother her. As soon as he'd found his feet and learned the routine, she would see as little of him as possible without jeopardising the patients.

At that moment Mrs Mack returned with an armful of

blankets and a pillow. Her eyes were slightly red, as if she'd been weeping.

Dr Cameron got to his feet and stood back to allow her and Fee to tuck blankets round the still unconscious figure. Carefully they rolled him onto his side and back again to slip a blanket beneath him.

Mrs Mack whispered, as she and Fee knelt either side of the Captain, 'What's going to happen, Nurse? The doctor's not going to send the captain away to the mainland, is he? I can look after him here just fine. I can make up a bed for him in the study. He always said that he wanted to die on Drummock.' Not realising the incongruity of the remark, she added, 'It would kill him to go to St Cath's to die.'

Fee knew exactly what she meant. Just as true islanders wanted their babies to be born on Drummock, so they all want to die there, although they were prepared to go to St Cath's for surgery or sophisticated treatments if necessary. But if nothing constructive could be done, they opted to remain in their own homes or go to their own little hospital unit in the town.

Tom was standing at one of the porthole-type windows with his back to the room, staring out at the green-blue sea. It was a fantastic view out across the Atlantic, and he could appreciate how the captain felt about his unusual home. No wonder he was something of a free spirit. A real old sea dog.

He hadn't heard much, but sensed the whispered conversation that Fee and the housekeeper were having. His own thoughts were not so divorced from theirs. It would be like going to prison for the old man to go into hospital on the mainland.

He'd noticed Mrs Mack's red eyes and guessed the cause. The old lady didn't want the captain to be sent to hospital. From out of his distant past, he recalled holidays in the Highlands with his grandparents, and could still remember the Highlanders' fierce independence.

He wished he hadn't upset Nurse McFie by seeming to accuse her of negligence. It was a million miles from the truth. She was obviously a dedicated nurse. She simply saw patients as people, not a collection of aches and pains and symptoms.

It had come out all wrong, not what he'd meant to say at all. But she fazed him with her cloud of fine red-gold hair which formed little ringlets and curls round her cheeks and temples. And the way that her wide blue-green eyes regarded him—the colour was much like the sea that he was staring at right now—had shaken him to the core. Sea-green eyes in such a nice face, open and smiling. It was a face one could trust.

Just as her patients trusted her. She was the expert on applied nursing and medicine on Drummock and he must persuade her that he accepted that. He had seen her in action, heard the compliments about her and noticed the genuine affection in which she was held. But every time he opened his mouth he seemed to offend her. It must be because they had got off to a bad start, looking as if he were sneaking into her territory. No wonder she found it hard to trust him.

He could murder those fools who had so mismanaged his arrival. Perhaps at some future date he would get the chance to clear himself with her. But right now he must talk to her about what to do for Captain Mackintosh. He just hoped that their views would coincide.

The clinical, impersonal doctor in him said loud and clear that he should send him to the mainland hospital for the latest high-powered physio and drug treatment,

however severe his stroke. But the logical step wasn't
necessarily the right one.

'Do you want me to give the captain oxygen?' Fee
asked.

Tom turned round with a jerk. 'Yes, please, do—
might make him more comfortable.' Comfortable but too
late, he thought, to restore those dying brain cells. The
latest thinking, a recent medical journal had reported,
was to blast a stroke case with oxygen and stimulants to
minimise brain damage. But to be realistic, the captain
had already been beyond that when he'd first seen him.

All the oxygen in the world wasn't going to revive
him or stave off the after-effects of a stroke of this se-
verity. Even if he recovered from the initial collapse, he
would be left with some degree of paralysis.

He watched as Fee deftly fitted the mask on the elderly, once handsome but now distorted face.

'When you've a moment, may we have a word?' he
said. 'Mrs Mack can keep an eye on the captain. The
poor old chap's not going anywhere just now, and the
kindest thing is to leave him be for the time being until
he can be moved safely.'

His comment took Fee by surprise. She'd thought he
would want to start pumping in adrenalin and other stimulants before moving him to the mainland. For that,
surely, was what he intended to do.

But if the captain was to be moved, there would be a
few hours in which to do it. The tiny islet on which The
Crow's Nest perched was connected to the main island
by a long spit of land, dry at low tide but under several
feet of water at high tide when a boat was the only
means of crossing to and fro. The tide at the moment
was still going out and the spit was dry. Of course, he

could be lifted by helicopter, but there wasn't a great deal of room to land a machine.

Reassuring Mrs Mack that they would remain within calling distance, they went out through a narrow door to the walkway that ran round the lighthouse tower. Tom and Fee stood just outside the porthole window so that Mrs Mack could see them and they could see her. The surf was churning up and down the beach a few yards away.

They both breathed in the salt-laced air with a sigh of pleasure.

'I suppose,' said Tom, lifting his face to the sun and closing his eyes, 'this is what one might call the magic of Drummock. My kids are already sold on it.'

That surprised her. Fee tried not to stare at his bronzed, handsome face, looking for the moment relaxed and happy. As she had once before, she experienced a touch of guilt because she had forgotten about his children. The expression on his face softened when he spoke of them.

His next words cut across her thoughts.

'What do you think we should do about the captain? It seems cruel to move him to the mainland. I think we both know there's only a one-in-a-million chance of improving his condition at his age.'

They were standing side by side, their hands resting on the safety rail that went round the walkway. He shifted one hand closer to hers, so that their little fingers were touching.

Goose-pimples sprang up on Fee's forearms, and she shivered in the warm sunshine.

Tom turned his head to look at her, and she turned hers at the same time and was dazzled by the brightness of his eyes.

For a moment their eyes remained locked, and then they both turned to look out across the sea. Tom moved his hand along the rail away from hers.

Fee took several deep breaths and tried to shake away the peculiar feeling the feather-light touch of his finger had produced. Nothing like this should happen to her. Sensible, practical Nurse McFie. Certainly not with Tom Cameron, whom she didn't even like.

She was clearing her throat to say something when Tom spoke again, picking up from where he'd left off as if nothing had happened. Nothing *has* happened, she assured herself.

'But if you think that the captain would want a chance to have high-tech treatment, we'll contact the air ambulance service and get him whisked over there at once.'

'It's the last thing he would want,' replied Fee, her voice husky but steady. 'He told me once that on no account was he to be moved to St Cath's if he got very ill, unless we couldn't manage him here. Gentleman that he is, he didn't want to be a burden to Mrs Mack or any of us, but he dearly wants to stay on Drummock, if possible.'

'Then let's get ourselves organised,' Tom ordered briskly. 'Let's get hold of your tame ambulance chappie and ask him to come over and help us move the captain to the hospital unit. Presumably you'll be able to staff it and cope with a heavy patient who's going to need turning regularly.'

Grateful to get back to talking shop, Fee nodded. 'There are enough nurses on standby to cover,' she assured him. 'Everyone will rally round. But it will mean overtime payments. I don't know how willing the authorities will be to underwrite this.'

There was a wicked gleam in his astonishingly blue

eyes, but his voice sounded grim. 'Leave that to me, Nurse, I'll sort it. They've already got a hell of a lot to answer for. They owe me and you.'

Fee's feet hardly touched the ground for the next few hours. She saw the captain, closely guarded by Mrs Mack, safely installed in the hospital, then arranged for a rota of nurses and helpers to cover the night and the following day's nursing. Finally excusing herself, she dashed off to take the afternoon surgery.

Already she was running half an hour late. Not that anyone would mind. They would all have heard about the captain's stroke.

She felt guilty leaving Tom Cameron to work out a programme of care for the patient with Jane Watters, the staff nurse who was on duty. She herself should have been there, doing it as a courtesy to him admitting his first patient to the hospital. Jane was, of course, perfectly able to deal with the matter, and she herself wouldn't be far away since the clinic block was only a short distance from the hospital proper. The trouble was, she had got so used to taking all the responsibility that she felt that she was neglecting her duty by not being there.

But was it only that? Was part of her reluctance to leave the hospital more personal? No! She squashed the embarrassing memory of her reaction to the touch of his hand when it had brushed hers. It was an incident that shouldn't have happened, a knee jerk reaction to a physically attractive man—that was all.

Halfway through the surgery she remembered that she'd meant to ask Tom if he wanted to sit in or take it over. But with all that had happened, it had completely flown out of her head. Oh, well, she would ask him if he wanted to do tomorrow's surgery.

She saw the last patient out at five o'clock and hurried over to the hospital unit to check on the captain.

Jane, all smiles, met her at the door.

'Dr Cameron went off soon after you did, after putting up a glucose and saline drip. He's pleased with the improvement that the captain's making. Just before he went, the old boy opened his eyes and obviously recognised Mrs Mack, so she's over the moon. She's helped me turn him a couple of times. She's tough as old boots, that one.'

'Yep, she's a grand old girl. Did you work out a routine for the Captain?'

Jane nodded. 'Half-hourly obs for the moment, slow controlled drip, replace with another bag of glucose and saline when necessary. Oral hygiene, of course, and pressure areas four-hourly. Oh, and the doctor put in a urinary catheter and wants us to keep a fluid balance chart.'

Fee frowned. 'We could have put in the catheter,' she said.

'Yes, I did say that I was willing to do it, but he said that as he was on the spot he might as well make himself useful.'

'Humph,' grunted Fee. 'Don't let him walk all over you, Jane. He'll be wanting to run the place if we're not careful.'

Jane grinned. 'Well, it's about time someone took some of the load off you.'

'Or does me out of a job altogether,' grumbled Fee, half seriously, half joking.

'Oh, I don't think that there's any danger of that,' said Jane. 'As well as being a gorgeous, handsome beast, I think he'll be pretty fair, as men go. We might have been lumbered with someone worse.'

'I wonder,' muttered Fee, as she went to look at the captain and have a word with Mrs Mack.

A few minutes later, she called goodbye to Jane. 'I'll be in again later, all being well.'

As she was leaving, Fee met Tom and his two children on the doorstep.

Completely taken by surprise, she said faintly, 'Oh.' She smiled rather uncertainly at the children. Unselfconsciously, they smiled back, looking incredibly like their father.

He said, 'Hi, I thought that I'd have another look see at the captain, and show the children round the unit. I like them to know where I'm working. I think it makes them feel more secure.' He laid a hand on the boy's head. 'This is Simeon, and this...' he transferred his large hand to the little girl's flaxen head '...is Philly.'

'My name is really Philomena,' said the pretty child, revealing a gap in her front teeth, 'but Daddy says that's a bit of a mouthful, so I'm called Philly for short.'

Fee recovered herself, and held out her hand to each of the children. 'My name's Fiona,' she said. 'But I'm always called Fee.'

'Can we call you Fee?' asked Simeon.

'Oh I don't think—' Tom started to say.

'Well, it is my name,' Fee butted in, warning him off with a quick shake of her head. 'Your father tells me that you're enjoying living on Drummock.'

'Yeah,' said Simeon enthusiastically. 'It's great. Do you know there's a miniature steam railway that goes round part of the island?'

Fee nodded. 'Yes, I used to go on it when I was a little girl.'

'Gosh, I didn't know it was that old,' said the boy.

Again Tom opened his mouth, obviously wanting to

apologise, but Fee only chuckled. 'My grandfather built it,' she explained. 'He was an engineer and built real railways all over the world.'

Simeon's eyes, as blue as his father's, sparkled. 'Wow,' he said. 'That's so cool.'

Philly hopped up and down on one foot. 'Yeah, real cool,' she said, obviously young enough to admire her elder brother.

Tom gave Fee a wry smile. 'You've made friends for life,' he said. 'Simeon's been hooked on steam trains ever since I first read him *Railway Stories*. And at the moment, where he leads, Philly happily follows.' He ruffled both small heads. 'That's right, kids, isn't it?'

Fee liked the way he didn't ignore the children but kept them in the conversation. They both looked up at him and then did a thumbs-up sign. It was obviously a ritual of some sort.

'Spot on, Dad,' said Simeon.

'Yeah, spot on,' agreed Philly.

CHAPTER FIVE

FEE drove the short distance home with her head full of mixed up thoughts. Surprise, irritation, embarrassment and even admiration for the excellent job Tom had made of bringing up his children chased round her tired brain. They were delightful kids. She was glad that she'd met them.

Her thoughts zoomed back to earlier in the day. She felt uncomfortable when she recalled her reaction to Tom Cameron's touch as they'd stood on the walkway of The Crow's Nest. Had he touched her deliberately? And, if so, why? Or was she reading a lot into a small, accidental episode? She sighed deeply. She would have gone along with that theory had it not been for the way their eyes had met and held for moments afterwards. *That* had not been accidental.

A frown creased her forehead. 'Oh, forget it, McFie,' she muttered. 'The man's obviously a charmer who knocks women over like ninepins. But you've got to work with him for the foreseeable future, and that's going to be difficult enough, without you behaving like a nervous filly. And maybe he feels as uncomfortable as you do about it and is wishing that he hadn't tried it on. So give the guy the benefit of the doubt. He's got a lot on his plate, with two kids to look after and a new job to tackle.'

Talking the situation through with herself out loud helped her to get matters in perspective. What it came down to was that, however reluctant she was to let him intrude into her territory, she must certainly rein in her anger when they were together. After all, they were both professionals, and should be able to maintain a professional front.

Let's just get through the next few weeks, she told herself as she pulled up in front of her house. Until we've sorted out our separate roles. Of course, there are going to be occasions when we'll have to work closely together, but I dare say we'll cope with that.

There was an e-mail waiting for her in her flat. It was from the chief medical administrator and was an apology for the delay in informing her of Dr Cameron's appointment.

Dear Miss McFie,

I understand that through a clerical error, you were not informed in good time, as you should have been, that Dr Thomas Cameron had been appointed Medical Officer to Drummock. Please accept my sincere apologies for this failure. I wish you and Dr Cameron a successful working partnership.

May I take this opportunity to thank you for all that you've done to cover the medical needs of the islanders in the interim.

Yours…

'Oh, yeah, and who are you kidding?' muttered Fee crossly. 'Clerical error, my foot! Talk about gilding the lily. You forgot I existed till someone reminded you. I wonder who that was? Tom Cameron himself probably. He was pretty steamed up about the way everything had gone haywire.'

Just as Fee got in late that evening from visiting a patient the phone rang. It was Margot McBain who was at the Forrester household. She was ringing to say that Blanche was through the transitional stage and into the second stage of labour.

'She's in good shape,' added Margot. 'I don't think that she's going to hang about. I believe she's going to have this baby as quickly and easily as she had the other two, in spite of how things started off this morning. And it's all down to you, Fee, managing to turn the babe around the way that you did. James can't stop singing your praises, and I must say I endorse what he says. You did a wonderful job, Fee. Not many obstetricians would have attempted what you did when labour had already started.'

Fee laughed a little self-consciously. It was almost embarrassing, hearing the often taciturn old midwife being so fulsome. 'Oh, well, you know what these husbands are once they think that the worst is over. Anyway, there really wasn't much choice. But from what you say, it sounds as if James will soon be able to have his best malt at the ready. I'll be with you in twenty minutes.'

'Och, that'll be fine. Now, can you ring Dr Cameron and let him know that we're near the finishing line? I did promise to keep him informed, and Blanche needs me to help her with pushing and panting right now.'

'Of course,' replied Fee, struggling to keep the chill note out of her voice at the mention of the doctor's name.

She was amazed and ashamed at how strongly she felt about Tom being present at the birth of Blanche's and James's baby. It was especially mean since she'd asked him to examine Blanche after she'd completed turning the baby.

But this was a Drummock birth and nothing to do with an outsider, she thought irrationally. And anyway, maternity cases traditionally belonged to the midwives. OK. So far he hadn't put a foot wrong in medical matters. He'd been kind and surprisingly understanding about his patient's feelings. In fact, he'd behaved pretty well impeccably. So why was she suddenly feeling resentful once again?

'How bitchy can you get, McFie?' she asked herself, as she punched in the number of Quay House.

She and Tom arrived at the Forresters' house at the same time. Tom driving up in a shiny new green Range Rover.

Fee whistled as she stepped out of her battered old vehicle. 'Very smart,' she said drily.

'She's a beauty, isn't she?' He smiled, patting the gleaming bodywork affectionately. 'Came over on today's ferry with the last of my luggage. I ordered it in Edinburgh on my way north, guessing it would be impossible to get around in the camper van on calls. Some of the lanes are too narrow to take it.'

He'd ordered it in Edinburgh! So he'd known then about the job. Which meant that the authorities had known about it, too. Oh, great! So much for the apologetic communication from the health authorities.

She reminded herself of the pep talk she'd given herself earlier and held onto her temper. It still wasn't his fault that she hadn't been informed of him coming.

With a little theatrical snort she said, 'Men and their cars! As long as it gets me from A to B, I don't think that it matters two hoots what it looks like,' lied Fee.

'You're jealous,' Tom grinned.

'You bet I am,' replied Fee, and from somewhere dug up a smile.

It had been a busy day, mused Fee as sleep evaded her in the early hours of the morning. She had got home from the Forrester house at half past twelve.

Blanche had given birth to a healthy baby boy weighing six and a half pounds at ten-thirty the previous evening. As Margot had predicted, it had been a smooth, straightforward delivery. In spite of the punishment her muscles had received earlier, she'd had good strong contractions, well controlled with help and advice from Margot, which she'd obeyed to the letter. In fact, Blanche had been a model patient.

Tom was introduced to the custom of wetting the baby's head with a wee dram of single malt as soon as possible after the baby had been born.

Fee had wondered if he would make any protest about drinking whilst on duty and later driving. The Forresters would have been very hurt had he refused. Had he done so, she would have pointed out that it was a centuries-old tradition, hadn't so far produced any accidents, as far as she knew, and, besides, the large wedge of real shortbread served with it was solid enough to soak up several drams.

But he hadn't refused. He had taken it in his stride, lifting his glass with the rest of them, and toasting the baby's health with a loud, 'Slainte!'

'What are you going to call the little lad?' he asked, touching the baby's head with a large gentle finger.

'Bruce,' Ian told him

'Bruce Forrester—it's got a nice solid ring to it,' he said, smiling down at Blanche. 'Congratulations, Mrs Forrester. You've come through everything with flying colours, in spite of the fright you gave us earlier on. Would you mind if I give you a quick examination after Midwife McBain has finished sorting you out, just to see if everything's as it should be?'

'Of course not. Please, call me Blanche. But I'm sure everything's all right, thanks to Fee.'

'So am I,' replied Tom with a smile. 'And as you say, it's thanks to Nurse McFie. She did a great job wrestling with that baby of yours.' He slid Fee a sideways grin.

Fee felt herself blushing and turned away to fiddle with something on the trolley, although there was nothing to do. It was Margot's delivery, and as always she had coped with her usual efficiency.

'Fee, why don't you go away home to your bed?' the old nurse suggested. 'You've had a beastie of a day, and there's nothing to keep you here. I can look after Dr Cameron.'

Of course she could look after Dr Cameron, Fee thought savagely later. Any woman would be glad to look after Tom Cameron, even sensible old Margot. He was quite simply a charmer, a dish, a hunk—whatever the latest word was to describe a bronzed giant with periwinkle blue eyes.

'No, that's not quite fair,' she scolded herself aloud, staring out at the starlit sky. 'There's a bit more to him than that.'

She wasn't quite sure why she was defending him, unless it had something to do with meeting his children. They seemed like lovely kids. He'd done a good job with them, though maybe that was all down to his late wife. How long ago had she died? Surely it couldn't have been too recently, because neither he nor Simeon and Philly seemed emotionally traumatised. Did she think that there was some depth in him because he'd followed her out of the Forrester house and endorsed what he'd already said about her skill in turning the baby? He hadn't needed to do that.

He'd obviously been sincere, praising her on a professional level as well as on a personal one. She couldn't help but be pleased. Then he'd stood in front of the house and closed her car door after she'd climbed in.

'Take care,' he'd said softly. 'Drummock needs you, Nurse McFie.'

It was a nice thought to go to sleep on.

But a ripple of regret assailed her as her eyelids drooped. She wished that she'd acknowledged his friendly wave as she'd driven away from the Forrester residence.

It was one-thirty a.m. when Tom arrived back at Quay House.

The house was in darkness except for the porch light, a dim light on the first floor landing and another in the ground-floor hall.

He let himself in quietly, then he came to a halt just inside the door. For a moment he stood stock still and stared speechlessly. Then he swore under his breath.

Simeon and Philly were sitting side by side on the stairs, bundled up in a duvet. Philly was asleep, her head on her brother's shoulder. The sound of snoring filtered down from upstairs.

Tom's heart turned over. What in the hell had happened? Why were the children down here and not safely tucked up in bed? He crossed the hall floor in three long strides and crouched down beside them, peering at them closely to see if they were all right.

His son looked up and put a finger to his lips. His

eyes, so like his father's, were bleary with tiredness but quite untroubled.

He smiled and whispered, 'We wanted to talk to you, Dad, but Philly fell asleep. We thought it would nice for you to have someone to talk to when you came home. Maggie said that you needed a wife to come home to so that you could talk about your work, and we thought, We could do that. But we didn't think you'd be quite so late.'

'But you're all right, son? Nothing's happened to upset you? No nightmares or anything?'

'Course not,' said Simeon scornfully. 'We don't have nightmares here on Drummock, not like we used to have.'

He sounded adult and secure, the frights of the past behind him. They had begun to diminish as they'd travelled north and seemed to have vanished within a few days of being on the island. As Fee had said, Drummock was safe for children.

Crouching down by them, Tom's heart nearly burst with pride. They'd had some nasty experiences over the last year or so, but they'd successfully toughed it out. He gave them a quick hug and stood up. His heart was still bumping unevenly from the fright he'd had when he'd first seen them, sitting like two little orphans at the foot of the stairs.

His legs felt decidedly wobbly. Long ago he'd heard the saying, 'Children maketh cowards of us all.' He thought at that moment how true it was.

There was a wonderful aroma of herbs drifting through from the kitchen. One of Maggie's stews at a guess.

He bent down and picked up Philly, gently easing her head from Simeon's shoulder. She remained fast asleep.

'Let's go along to the kitchen,' he suggested softly. 'We'll make Philly comfortable in the big armchair, and you and I can have a chat.' It was time, he thought, that he and his son got to know each other a bit better. There hadn't been time or opportunity before.

He must also, without seeming to probe, find out a bit about Maggie Shillington. As far as he could see, though he had only employed her for such a short while, she was a gem of a housekeeper, a great cook and wonderful with the kids. But he really knew little about her. He had taken her solely on trust, because she appeared to go with the practice and had been employed by his predecessor. And although they hadn't talked about it much, Nurse McFie seemed to think it a good arrangement, and he trusted her judgement.

Quay House was already beginning to feel like home, and that was largely down to Maggie's presence. The kitchen was always full of aromatic scents, whilst the rest of the house smelt of lavender polish. Yet she wasn't so houseproud as to scold the children if they came into the kitchen with dirty feet.

'Och,' he'd heard her say several times when they'd apologised, 'Away with you. A wee bitty of dirt is nae difficult to clean.'

In fact, he thought ruefully, they were in danger of being spoilt by Maggie. But she had definitely blotted her copybook tonight by sleeping through the children getting up and coming downstairs. It didn't bode too well for nights when he might be called out once he was in full-time practice, and that was only days away. Something would have to be done about it, but he wasn't sure what.

All these thoughts tumbled through Tom's mind as he carried Philly along the corridor, with Simeon bringing up the rear, trailing the duvet. Carefully, he lowered his small daughter into the vast armchair so as not to wake her, and moved back to give Simeon room to tuck the duvet over her.

The sight of his son, frowning in concentration as he gently wrapped the quilt round his sister, brought a lump to Tom's throat.

The boy had grown up so quickly in the last few months, and had become so protective of Philly after the horrors of the past year or so.

Since coming to Scotland and especially to Drummock, there had been a change in both children. They were blossoming again, happy and carefree, as they should be, and actually looking forward to going to their new school.

That was something of a miracle, after the battles he'd had with them to go to school when they'd lived in the city. And there had been no nightmares since they'd arrived on Drummock, which might be termed another small miracle.

Tom asked Simeon if he was hungry.

'Starving,' replied Simeon.

'What did you have for supper?' asked Tom, wondering a little uneasily if Maggie was a bit off colour, and unusually, hadn't fed them properly.

Simeon's face lit up. 'Two huge duck eggs, like this,' he said, demonstrating their size with his hands. 'Well, I had two, Philly could only manage one. They were delicious and we collected them ourselves from Maggie's ducks.'

Clearly Maggie hadn't neglected them at all. He shouldn't have doubted her. After all, Fee had given her the OK. 'She can be an old besom,' she'd said, 'but loyal to the core. She'll never let you down.'

His son was simply starving because he was seemingly growing inches taller a day, though he was still as
lean as a greyhound.

Tom grinned. 'I was always hungry at your age,' he
said, filling two bowls with stew.

They both attacked the stew hungrily and in a friendly
silence. For some reason Tom found himself thinking of
Fee McFie, and of its own volition a picture popped into
his head of her sitting at the table with them.

A little fantasy unfolded itself in his tired mind. Fee
was sitting at the other end of the table, nursing a baby.
Of course, he had seen her nursing baby Bruce a couple
of hours ago and had thought how it suited her. Idly he
wondered why an attractive woman like her hadn't married and had children of her own, instead of delivering
other women's babies. It didn't seem possible that no
one had asked her. Perhaps one day it would happen,
and she would confide in him when she got to know the
kids better. It was a shame she was still so uptight about
his arrival on Drummock. He would have to work on
her some more.

She was a remarkable woman, and a super nurse, able
to turn her hand to virtually anything in the medical line.
A natural healer. He wasn't sure that he would have had
the nerve to turn the Forrester baby once labour had
started, even if it had been early on.

'There's apple tart in the larder, Dad, and a jug of
custard.' Simeon's voice broke in on his thoughts. 'Shall
I get it?'

'Why not?' said Tom. 'I think I could find a corner.'
Then, suddenly remembering that the children had met
Fee the previous afternoon, he added casually, 'What did
you think of Nurse McFie, Simmy? She's rather nice,
isn't she?' He hoped that the children had liked her.

'We *thought* she was,' replied Simeon, concentrating on cutting two huge slices of tart.

Tom's heart sank at the note of reservation in the boy's voice.

'*Thought?*' he repeated. 'You don't sound very sure.'

Simeon pushed a pudding plate and the jug of custard across the table. He waited until Tom had added a little custard to his tart and returned the jug, then poured a generous helping onto his own plate. 'Well, you see,' he said thoughtfully, 'Maggie says that the nurse doesn't like us very much. She thinks that we'll be a drag on you when you work.'

Tom lowered his spoon from his lips. Fee couldn't have said that, could she? It didn't sound like her. Yet why should his housekeeper say that she had? There must be some mistake or the children had misinterpreted. 'And when did Maggie drop these pearls of wisdom?' he asked, trying to keep his tone light and amusing.

'Last night when we came back from the hospital and told her that we had met the nurse. It was when you were in your study. And then you were on the phone for ages so we couldn't tell you. I don't mind if she does think we're a drag, but Philly didn't like it. It made her think of that last nanny we had in London. She used to say that…and all sorts of other things.'

He shovelled more tart and custard into his mouth, his cheeks bulging. Tom knew that he should remind him of his table manners, but he hadn't the heart. Blow table manners—it was a joy to see Simeon eating properly again. He didn't want to think of those last months in his inner-city practice and the succession of unsuitable nannies he had employed.

That must never happen again, especially not here on beautiful Drummock. Nobody was going to make his children miserable. From now on he was going to fill their days with happiness.

'Were those the exact words that Maggie used? Did she say that Nurse McFie referred to you as a drag?'

Simeon put the last spoonful into his mouth and masticated it slowly. His small brow beetled. 'I'm not sure,' he mumbled through a mouthful of pastry. 'But it was something like that. Anyway, that's what she meant.' He pushed his plate aside, folded his arms on the table and lowered his head. 'Gosh, I'm tired,' he said.

Fee arrived at the surgery at seven-thirty next morning, and found Tom leaning against his gleaming Range Rover, reading a newspaper.

Oh, no! She had hoped that today would be free of emergencies and free of the doctor for, although he was officially Medical Officer, his appointment had only been brought forward to enable him to help out the previous day and he should still be on holiday. Surely he owed it to his children to spend time with them before he started work properly and they started school.

He seemed to read her mind for he folded his paper and said evenly, 'I won't keep you long, Nurse. I've promised the children that we'll explore the island properly today, but I'd like to fix a time and date to have an in-depth discussion about our future working rota.'

'An in-depth discussion?' Fee repeated blankly.

The doctor frowned. 'Well, surely you've thought about it!' His voice was brusque. 'I can hardly turn up to take surgery on Monday without some preparation. And we need to sort out visits. I must know when I can call on you or other nurses who are available to visit patients or do dressings or whatever.'

His blue eyes were suddenly steely. 'Or am I denied

the services of your nursing staff except in emergencies? I've only met the staff nurse at the hospital unit and Midwife McBain. I would rather like an opportunity to meet the other nurses and anyone else connected with the medical services on Drummock. I'd be grateful if you could arrange that as soon as possible, please.'

It was his icy politeness that struck home. Whatever had happened to the warmth with which he had told her to drive carefully when he'd seen her off from the Forresters' last night? Had it really upset him that she hadn't acknowledged his goodbye wave? Was he really that sensitive? It was absurd.

The chilliness with which she had treated him was nothing compared with his iciness. Fee went pale and then her cheeks blazed a fiery red and she put a hand to her throat. He was all but accusing her of deliberately withholding information from him, and making it abundantly clear that there was going to be a marked division between doctor and nurses in the future. And guess who would be the boss?

Her conscience nudged her. She hadn't deliberately held anything back but she'd certainly not gone out of her way to make things easy for him. In that she was at fault. She should have arranged a meeting with the key health people to meet him before he was due to start work. It would have been a natural courtesy.

She fumbled as she tried to unlock the surgery door to give herself time to come up with a sensible answer. 'Do come in,' she said, urging him forward as she would a visitor.

He took a few long strides across the cobbled pavement, but he didn't allow her to usher him through in front of her. Instead, he put his hand on the small of her back and impatiently pushed her through the doorway.

It wasn't in the least a sexy gesture, rather an exasperated one.

Fee's pulse rate rose as anger surged through her. OK,
she had made mistakes, she should have handled the
whole business of his arrival better, but really! She
wouldn't argue with him, or offer any excuses or reasons
for what he saw as her keeping him out in the cold and
only calling on him when she'd needed him. She crossed
straight to the desk and opened the page-a-day diary and
turned to the following day.

'What about—?' she started to say, when he stopped
her by putting a hand over hers.

'Is it true,' he grated, 'that you think that my children
are an encumbrance, a drag, and that you'll end up doing
more than your fair share of the work.'

How could he have thought that of her? Again her
cheeks flushed and paled as her pulse skyrocketed. It was
becoming a habit only associated with the doctor. She
must hold onto her temper and refrain from grinding her
teeth.

'I wouldn't dream of labelling any child a drag,' she
spat out. 'However difficult they are. They're not all
angelic, but why should they be? They're a mixed bag,
as their parents are. And as it happens, your children
struck me as being very well…adjusted. They were
cheerful and polite.'

His voice and eyes were glacial. 'What do you mean,
"well adjusted"?'

What an extraordinary reaction to a well-meant com-
pliment.

It was too late to withdraw the remark so she might
as well be honest and direct. 'I mean that they seem to
have recovered from losing their mother remarkably
well. It must be the biggest trauma that children have to

survive—the loss of a parent. I'm sorry if for some reason you found the comment offensive.'

He stood by the desk, staring out of the window. His face had a closed look about it. After a moment or two of silence, he said, 'I'm not offended, just afraid for my children.'

'Understood,' replied Fee, though, in fact, she only partly understood.

Why was his wife's death shrouded in mystery? And did it link up with why he was so angry because he thought she'd referred to them as a drag? Had his wife thought of them as an encumbrance? Her years of nursing had taught her that many seemingly happy marriages held dark secrets. Was Dr Cameron's one of them?

But none of this answered the question of how he had got hold of the idea that she had declared his kids a drag and was afraid that he wouldn't pull his weight. If anything, she was afraid that he would be too pushy and work too hard.

Swallow your pride and apologise again for the misunderstanding, she told herself.

She produced a tight smile. 'Well, it looks as if somewhere along the line we got our wires crossed,' she said. 'Shall we put the mix-up behind us and get on with our lives?'

He nodded, but still looked grim. 'Seems like a good idea,' he agreed.

Fee turned to the next page in the diary. 'What about tomorrow afternoon for the meeting?' she suggested. 'I'll round up as many people as possible and we can have it here. There isn't an afternoon surgery or clinic.'

'That suits me,' said Tom. 'What time?'

'Two thirty,' said Fee.

Tom slightly inclined his head. 'Right. See you then.'
Lifting his hand, he let himself out of the office, leaving
it feeling very empty indeed.

CHAPTER SIX

FOR several minutes after Tom had gone, Fee sat staring at the door, filling it in her imagination with his commanding figure.

Commanding and authoritative, but right now looking vulnerable. It had come over loud and clear. He was so scared for his children that he couldn't bear to have them criticised as he thought she had done. Which brought her to the thorny question of who had planted the idea in his mind that she'd suggested that they might prove to be a stumbling block in the practice.

She raked her memory to see if at any point in the short time since he'd arrived on the island she had said anything that could have been remotely construed as a criticism of the Cameron children. Patients and nurses had quizzed her about him since day one, but she'd purposely avoided any in-depth conversations with anyone, saying quite truthfully that she didn't know much about him.

The only person she'd talked to at any length about the matter had been...Maggie Shillington. Oh, no! Had she been indiscreet? Maggie was such a fixture it was easy to let one's guard down. She often dropped in on Maggie halfway through her rounds for a cup of coffee.

Fee trawled her memory. Had she made a remark about the doctor having a young family that might interfere with his work? The possibility had been in her thoughts, but had she voiced them aloud? She had been so incensed about the doctor's sudden presence on

Drummock that she might have let her tongue run away
with her. But she didn't think so. Even in her anger she
was too automatically professional to let drop such a
remark.

She shrugged. She couldn't resolve the problem for
the moment, so she put it from her mind and pulled the
appointments book toward her and checked the list of
patients already booked in to see her. There were ten,
and she guessed that probably half of them were simply
curious to know more about the new man.

Kirsty, the nurse-receptionist, confirmed that this was
true. 'The phone's been going mad,' she said with a wide
grin. 'Amazing how many people have developed gastric
symptoms since yesterday.'

'Then I'm surprised that there aren't more to see,'
replied Fee.

Laughter bubbled up in Kirsty's throat. 'Oh, astonishingly enough, some of them actually recovered while
they were speaking to me, after I told them that he
wasn't taking surgery till Monday. I bet he'll be inun-
dated then.'

'Poor man,' said Fee, her eyes bright with laughter.
'What a baptism. We'd better warn him.'

The surgery was straightforward.

Greg Rogers was first in. He had a nasty boil on the
small of his back just above the crease in his buttocks.
He was a keen cyclist, which perhaps had something to
do with it—shorts rubbing against sweaty skin, or something. Fee explained that the boil needed to be cleaned
up and covered, and she would start him on a course of
antibiotics to deal with the underlying infection.

'And next week I...' she remembered the medicine
man would be at work '...or Dr Cameron will lance it

under a local anaesthetic and it will heal up nicely,' she added.

Greg was a good-looking seventeen-year-old with a growing reputation for attracting girls by the score. He admitted he was more concerned about whether he would end up with an ugly scar than caring about the discomfort he was feeling.

Fee covered the inflamed lump with a magnesium sulphate dressing, which, though an old-fashioned treatment, still worked well by drawing the septic matter into a small area, then said, 'Does it matter? After all, it won't be all that visible once it's healed. It'll be covered by your clothes.'

Greg went brick red and mumbled something about girlfriends seeing it.

Hiding a smile, Fee said, 'I bet it will take more than a little scar to put them off you, Greg.'

His blush began to subside. 'Honest, Nurse?' he asked, suddenly very young and unsure of himself.

'Scout's honour,' she replied, saluting with two fingers.

'Thanks,' he said with a smile that would break any female heart.

For some reason the smile reminded her of Tom Cameron.

'Don't forget to make an appointment with Kirsty for the surgical session next week,' she said as he was on his way out. 'And thank your lucky stars that I'm not a cradle-snatcher,' she added under her breath. 'You're going to be lethal in a few years' time.'

Her next patient, Mrs McNabb, was a crony of Maggie Shillington's. She was complaining of vague abdominal pain and a feeling of nausea. Fee's first thought was that she was doing a bit of Nosy-Parkering about

Dr Cameron, but realised that she didn't need to do that with Maggie as a confidante. And hadn't there been something in her record a few months ago about abdominal pain? Fee seemed to recall old Dr Franks debating whether to send her to St Cath's for investigation.

Fee switched on the monitor and brought up Alice McNabb's medical records. Yes, there it was. Almost six months ago Alice had come to the surgery complaining of vague abdominal pain, and that hadn't been the first time. According to the notes, Dr Franks had decided that she was probably suffering from chronic constipation. She had very little fibre in her diet. He had prescribed a course of Fybogel and had asked her to come back in a fortnight. There was no record of her having returned.

'Will you get undressed, please, Mrs McNabb? I'd like to examine you.' Fee gestured to the curtained couch.

'I thought that you could just give me some of that stuff that the old doctor prescribed. It worked a treat.'

'I might do that,' Fee agreed patiently, 'but I'd still like to feel your tummy first.'

Mrs McNabb pursed her lips. 'Perhaps I should wait and see the new doctor,' she said. 'After all, he's a *real* doctor.' She patted Fee's arm. 'Och, you've done very well, lass, since the old one left, but doctoring's not really your job, is it? You're only a nurse when all's said and done.'

It was the 'only' that hurt. Fee had always wanted to be a nurse. Her parents had said, 'Why not be a doctor?' As her teachers at school had. One of them had suggested that it was a waste of good A-levels.

'But I don't want to be a doctor,' she'd replied patiently. 'I want to be a nurse and good A-levels are just as necessary for that. Nowadays nursing isn't only about bedpans and bed baths, it's also about understanding drugs and knowing when and how to give them. Besides, nursing will keep me closer to the patients, which is what I want.'

And now she wanted to scream out all that to this nasty old woman, who must have known that Fee had been taking on more and more responsibility over the last couple of years even whilst old Dr Franks had still been practising. She wanted to say that it had taken her years to obtain all her qualifications—nearly as long as it took a doctor to qualify. But she knew better than to do that. It would cut no ice with Mrs McNabb in the mood she was in and she mustn't drive the woman away without giving her a lifeline.

All Fee's instincts told her that, in spite of the old lady's feistiness, there was something really wrong with her. And she remembered having thought that when Alice had visited the surgery six months before.

She hadn't accepted Dr Franks's almost casual diagnosis of constipation, believing that there were underlying reasons for the constipation besides an inadequate diet. But he had been in one of his stubborn moods, which had become increasingly frequent by that time, and wouldn't be persuaded that he should send Mrs McNabb to the mainland for further investigations.

'We'll wait and see,' he'd said.

Now Fee felt strongly that they shouldn't wait any longer. She had a nasty feeling that something was very wrong. A lot could have happened in six months. Most of it was instinctive, but there were faint but visible signs that all was not well with the old lady. There was a slight sheen of sweat on her face, her eyes were dull and she was agitated—all of which had been concealed when she'd first arrived because of her normal sprightliness.

Fee took a deep breath to restore her calm and then said evenly, 'All right Mrs McNabb, if you don't trust me to examine you, that's your choice. But I'm not sure how soon a doctor can get over from the mainland and I really think that you should be examined by someone without delay.' She didn't want to sound alarmist but she had to get through to this stubborn, elderly patient somehow.

'What about the new man, then? Maggie says that he's very good.'

Silently Fee ground her teeth. 'He is,' she replied, 'but he doesn't start work until Monday.' Which was no longer true, she realised, since he had pulled strings to be present at the birth of the Forrester baby's birth.

'He saw Mrs Cox and the captain, *and* young Blanche and her new wee bairn.'

Fee gentled her voice. 'They were all emergencies,' she said. And then the thought struck her with extraordinary clarity that if Alice wasn't seen very soon, she, too, would be an emergency.

Swallowing her last vestiges of pride, Fee reached the decision that she must contact Tom Cameron. 'I believe he's going to take his children out for the day,' she said, reaching for the phone, 'but I'll see if I can catch him and have a word with him. If you'd like to go back to the waiting room, Mrs McNabb...' She indicated the door.

It was the last thing that Alice wanted to do but seeing the expression on Fee's face and realising that she'd got what she wanted, she rose to leave.

'Mrs McNabb,' called Fee as she reached the door,

'don't broadcast this to everyone, please, or they'll all want preferential treatment.'

Preferential treatment! Alice liked the sound of that and certainly didn't want anyone sharing it with her.

'My lips are sealed, Nurse,' she said.

The Cameron family were on the point of leaving the house when she phoned. Embarrassed at having to ask Tom for help yet again, Fee didn't try for finesse, but said bluntly when he picked up the receiver, 'Could you possibly see a patient today? It's a Mrs Alice McNabb...' She gave him a succinct account of the patient's condition, and with a little more difficulty explained why she thought that Alice should be seen as soon as possible. 'It's nothing that I can put my finger on exactly,' she said. 'It's just—'

'Your famous instinct at work,' Tom finished for her.

'Yes.' She was relieved that he didn't sound cross or sarcastic.

'Where do you want me to see her?'

'Wherever it suits you best. It could be here at the surgery or at—'

There was a knock at the door and it was opened briskly by Kirsty. Muttering an apology, she rushed to the washbasin, grabbed a stainless-steel bowl from beside it and said as she bustled back to the door, 'Mrs McNabb's being sick. Says it's happened several times.' Then she was gone again.

Tom said patiently, 'You've obviously got a crisis on. I'll see Mrs McNabb at her house at around midday.'

'The crisis concerns Mrs M. She's just vomited and apparently has done it before, but she didn't mention it when she gave me her history.'

There was a hissed intake of breath from Tom, and then he said, 'Puts a different complexion on it, and endorses your instinctive reaction. If you can get her across to the hospital, I'll see her there in fifteen minutes. I'll have to sort out the kids first.'

'Oh, dear, they'll be so disappointed. They thought that they were going to have you to themselves. I could deal with this myself, which is what I would do if you weren't here, but as I've explained, Alice is being difficult. Please, apologise to your children for me.'

'I will, but don't worry—they're used to it. At least, they were.'

Mrs McNabb made no protest as she was moved to the hospital, undressed and popped into bed.

Fee had to hurry back and finish her surgery. She handed the frightened old lady over to Staff Nurse Jane Watters. Surprisingly, Alice seemed reluctant for Fee to go.

'I'll come back later,' Fee promised, 'when I've finished surgery.'

'You won't let them send me away,' begged Alice. All the fight seemed to have left her.

Being pretty sure that this was exactly what would happen unless he considered it already too late, Fee said gently, 'Dr Cameron will do what he thinks is best, Alice. You'll be safe with him.' She had never used Alice's first name to her face, but it just slipped out. Poor old thing, she was frightened and vulnerable.

Fee put her arms round the thin shoulders. '*If* you have to go to St Cath's for investigations, it'll only be for a short time and then you can come back here to be looked after.'

'Promise me?' quavered Alice, now seeming infinitely pathetic.

'I promise,' said Fee, her heart heavy, knowing that

Alice would only be away a short time. She had the feeling that the old lady was deteriorating fast right in front of her eyes.

It was an uncanny feeling, stronger than anything that she'd had before.

Outside the ward door she leaned against the wall and closed her eyes. She couldn't believe what she and Jane had found when they'd undressed Alice. Her abdomen was swollen to twice the size that it should have been and was as taut as a drum. It had been concealed under layers of clothes and a heavy winter coat. Everywhere else she was as thin as a rake.

All this had happened in the last six months, for even Dr Franks, failing as he had been by then, couldn't have missed this.

'You've had a shock,' said Tom from close beside her.

Fee hadn't heard him approach. Like many large men, he was soft-footed. Her eyes flew open. He was frowning, a concerned expression on his face.

'Yes, I have,' she replied. 'It's Alice McNabb. I told you that she wouldn't let me examine her?'

He nodded.

'Well, now I know why and I'm not surprised. Something pretty horrific is going on. No wonder the poor old thing is scared stiff. Her abdomen is badly swollen...well, you'll see for yourself.' Fee waved her hand toward the ward. 'Look, I must go, I've a surgery full of people waiting to be seen. But Jane has all the notes, she'll fill you in. I'll catch up with you as soon as I can.'

'Don't worry,' Tom said and, answering her unspoken request, added, 'I won't do anything dramatic until we've discussed it.'

'That's very good of you,' she answered stiffly, wondering how it was that he seemed to be able to read her mind, and finding it a rather uncomfortable sensation.

The surgery seemed endless. There were no more scares that day. There were a few time-wasters but most patients had genuine problems. Several remarked on how lucky they were now to have a doctor on the island, but they didn't say it with malice.

A couple of patients expressed similar opinions to those of Ian McKay's, and hoped that she wouldn't feel pushed aside now that there was a doctor around. One of them declared that she would still rather see Fee and hoped that would still be possible.

'Especially,' she murmured shyly, 'when it's a woman's problem. Men just don't understand.'

She was just starting the menopause, and was supersensitive about hot flushes and all the other unpleasant side effects of the hormonal changes that had hit her.

Fee said reassuringly. 'I'm sure that you'll find Dr Cameron very understanding. And he may well be willing to let me keep tabs on you. I'll have a word with him.'

It is a good idea, she thought as she tidied up, for the women to still see me if they wanted to. I'll try to talk him round.

And perhaps it would help to take the edge off losing the medical side of the practice.

She sped over to the hospital as soon as she'd finished in the surgery. She expected Tom would be long gone, but he was just leaving and she met him in the doorway.

'Alice—how is she?' she asked breathlessly.

He edged her into the little office just inside the door. 'Not good,' he said softly. 'Her blood pressure has dropped through the floor and the retention of urine is

making a manual examination difficult. God knows
what's happening to her kidneys or bladder. I've re-
leased some of the urine and have left a catheter *in situ*,
with instructions to Staff Nurse to release a few mil at
quarter-hourly intervals. I don't want to risk her going
into shock.'

'Do you think her kidneys are still functioning?'

'Hard to tell. Staff has started a fluid balance chart
and I've put up a glucose drip with a painkiller in it. I'm
reluctant to do anything more dramatic until I know
more. I want to examine her bowels but she's in too
much distress at the moment. Anyway, I'll be back in a
short while to do a rectal on her and then we'll decide
what's got to be done. Now I must go and check up on
the kids.'

'Poor things. I hope that it doesn't put them off living
on Drummock, having you torn away from them at short
notice.'

He said, 'Are you kidding? They're having the time
of their lives. They're out with Maggie's brother on a
trip round the harbour in his boat. If we were back in
London they would be miserable as hell and it would
take me days to shake them out of it.'

'Oh, I'd forgotten about Maggie's brother and his
boat. I'm so glad they've had something to do to make
up for you working.'

Tom chuckled. It was a deep, rich chuckle that
matched his wide smile. There was warmth there and…

He was saying something but she hadn't really taken
it in. 'I'm sorry,' she said. 'What did you say?'

His eyes were amused. 'I was just commenting on the
number of relatives that Maggie has scattered around.'

'All true Drummers have loads of relatives scattered
around,' she replied, 'so you'd better be cautious about

the sort of remarks you make about anybody. We're very clannish here.'

'Have you a lot of relatives scattered around, Fee?'

Fee! He'd called her by her first name for the first time. It sounded different, coming from him. 'Dozens,' she replied with a smile, 'so take care, Dr Cameron.'

'Tom!' he answered, still smiling. He opened the door a fraction. 'I won't be long, and then we'll do what we can to sort out poor old Alice.'

Fee gave herself a few minutes to pull herself together when Tom had left. He really had gone out of his way to be pleasant and not make a big thing out of her having to call him. She was grateful for that, but she mustn't overdo the gratitude or let it run away with her. She would try to live up to her self-made promise to be seen to be friendly with him, if only for the sake of the patients, but no more than that.

Today's surgery had illuminated again the different attitudes of the islanders—how some seemed to welcome him with open arms and others to almost resent his presence. It was strange how quickly they had begun to take sides, even before most of them had met him. Rumour, of course, was always rife on Drummock as it was in any close community, and in her capacity as nurse-practitioner she had always been aware of it and managed to steer clear of becoming involved.

But this time it was almost impossible as she was part of the rumour. Several people had asked her directly how she felt about having a doctor brought in over her head, and she had been hard put to answer without revealing her bitter, angry feelings. Generally she said something like, 'It's very nice to have someone to share the load with.' Or, 'It'll be a relief not to have to call over a doctor from the mainland.'

Not everyone was deceived. One old chap actually said that she was a braw lass to put a brave face on things—'like your ma would have done,' he'd added—but it couldn't be easy.

Jane tapped on the office door. 'The captain heard that you were around,' she said, 'and is making it known through Mrs Mack that he wants to see you. He's incredible. When he came in, we thought that he was at death's door, but obviously he doesn't intend to go just yet.'

Fee grinned. 'Dr Cameron thought that he wouldn't last more than a few hours, which is why he didn't send him over to St Cath's.'

The staff nurse grinned back. 'He didn't know the powers ranged on the captain's side—Mrs Mack at her most formidable. She hasn't let the old boy rest, hasn't stopped talking to him.' She laughed out loud. 'I don't think he dared to let himself die.'

Fee sobered suddenly. 'I only wish that she could do the same for Alice McNabb, but I'm afraid that Alice is beyond even Mrs Mack's powers,' she said.

'Yep, 'fraid you're right,' said Jane sadly. She looked at her watch. 'Time to go and do her obs. I've left Di sitting with her.'

'Di from the laundry?'

'That's right. I'd forgotten she's Alice's cousin. She was just going off duty and heard that she'd been admitted, so offered to stay a bit and sit with her. She's going to let some of the others in the family know, too, so there'll probably be hordes of them here later.'

And I wonder what the good doctor will think of that, mused Fee as she followed Jane.

* * *

The good doctor didn't appear to think anything of it, except to be rather pleased.

'Do her good to know that the family's rooting for her. Best medicine in the world, as long as they let her rest in between. I always worry more for people who haven't got family back-up.'

They reached Alice's bedside. She was dozing and looking less haggard than she had an hour earlier.

'What a difference a painkiller, warmth and a little tender loving care can do.' Tom smiled at Di. 'I understand that you're a cousin,' he said.

'That's right, I'm Di McNabb,' she confirmed. 'I'm one of Alice's cousins, but I've always called her Aunty. It was a shock to hear that she was in here. I've never seen her in bed before, she's a fierce old thing. Can you tell me how she's doing, Doctor?'

How much should he tell her? Where did she come in the relatives' hierarchy? Tom looked at the tall, attractive woman standing on the other side of the bed. She was around forty, he guessed, with a wealth of the reddish-gold hair that seemed to typify many of the women of Drummock.

He cast a lightning-fast glance at Fee standing beside her. Her hair was almost the same colour, but of a quite different texture—fine and light and only just constrained by a wide band keeping it back from her face.

Di's hair was thick and heavy and coiled elaborately on top of her head. It struck Tom that she was a most unlikely laundry lady, another Drummock surprise.

She looked regal, calmly waiting for his answer. Did it really matter which member of the family he talked to about Alice's condition? This wasn't London and everyone would know soon enough anyway. He was pretty sure that there wouldn't be good news.

Fee divined his thoughts and nodded slightly. Go on, her eyes told him, do what you think is right. You're in Drummock now and you don't need to worry about red tape.

Gently he said, 'Well, I'll be able to tell you more when I've finished examining her. If you would be kind enough to wait outside for a few minutes, I'll not be long.'

Ten minutes later, Fee pulled back the curtains that had been drawn round the bed and smiled at the waiting Di.

'We're all finished,' she said.

Tom had been bending over the bed, talking quietly to Alice, but he patted her shoulder and straightened up as Fee finished drawing back the curtains. He moved over to where Di was waiting.

'Let's go along to the office,' he said, taking her arm. Once in the office he continued gently, 'I'm afraid that your cousin—aunt—has a growth of some sort in her bowel.'

Di looked him straight in the eye. 'You mean she's got cancer?'

'We won't know until she has various scans and tests.'

'That means that she'll have to go to the mainland.'

'Yes, but she might not be there for more than a few days.'

'But they'll want to operate, whatever they find, won't they Doctor?'

'Possibly.'

'You mean, unless it's too far advanced to do anything about it, which is quite likely in my aunt's case?'

Honesty was the best policy. 'I can't answer that directly right now. I need to talk to Nurse McFie,' he said. 'She's familiar with local procedures and will have a better idea how to go about moving Mrs McNabb to St Cath's.'

Di stood up. 'Dr Cameron.' Her voice was cool and steady. 'I'm sorry you've been landed with this problem. You know that if there had been a proper doctor on the island for Alice to see, something might have been done for her months ago.'

She slid on her shoulder-bag and started to move toward the door. Tom stood up uncertainly.

'True, Alice is a stiff-necked old besom and should have consulted Fee,' Di said as she paused at the door. 'But she's one of the oldies who thought that Dr Franks could do no wrong and it would have been a slight to him if she saw Fee. She knew fine that Fee had been running things for months before he went but wouldn't admit it, so she waited until a proper doctor appeared before showing up at the surgery.'

She had her hand on the doorknob.

'Personally I think that Fee McFie is the best. She knows her stuff, whether it's medicine or nursing. For her sake I wish things were different. But if it turns out that because there wasn't a doctor for Alice to see nothing can be done for her, my family will sue the authorities.'

CHAPTER SEVEN

DI MCNABB'S ominous warning hung in the air. Were they empty words? Tom didn't think so.

He stared out of the small window overlooking the ward. He could see Fee talking to Alice. Even at a distance she conveyed a caring quality he thought. It wasn't fair that she should be penalised for doing more than her share for the people of Drummock, for shouldering more than her responsibility for cases like this. Not that Di would involve her unnecessarily—that was for sure—but it was inevitable that Fee's name would crop up.

Tom took a deep breath. And it's not fair on me either he acknowledged, being dragged into the politics of medicine before I've had time to put a stethoscope to my ears. Just because Fee had the guts to ask for my help, which must have been galling for her, and I was only too ready to jump in, now we're both being dumped on.

Well, the sooner I put her into the picture, the better.

Fee was much less bothered than Tom had thought she would be when she joined him in the office and he related what had happened. He wondered if she thought he was exaggerating.

'Miss McNabb meant it, you know,' he said.

'Oh, I'm sure she did,' Fee replied easily. 'Di's a fighter and has a quick temper. Well, it won't hurt the powers that be to have their cage rattled. I've been wanting to do it for ages. Now, shall we have a cup of tea while we talk about how we can help Alice? Or do you want to get away for the children?'

He shook his head. 'No to having to collect the kids—they're going back with Maggie's brother for tea. They've taken lunch with them on the boat—pasties and doorstep sandwiches made by Maggie. They've both acquired enormous appetites since we've been here. All this fresh air and sunshine, I suppose. So I'm surplus to requirements at present and, I can tell you, that's a weight off my mind after...' He paused, staring into the middle distance for a moment, and then said, 'And yes, please, to a cup of tea. I could murder one.'

Fee disappeared for a moment into the tiny kitchen behind the office to fill and plug in the kettle, and to wonder what it was that he had seen in his mind's eye. Ghosts of some sort, she guessed. She was surprised at how sad he'd looked when he'd related his conversation with Di. Somehow she hadn't expected him to be bothered by such a matter. It was rather disappointing. She'd thought him made of sterner stuff.

She returned with a plateful of gingerbread which she pushed toward him. 'It's delicious,' she said. 'Courtesy of Mrs Mack. She went home for an hour or so to fetch some things for the captain, and knocked this up while she was there.'

He took a large chunk of gingerbread and began to eat hungrily. 'Forgot lunch,' he said apologetically.

'So did I,' said Fee.

She had sent Jane to lunch and had meant to go herself when the staff nurse returned, but had been busy when Jane had come back an hour ago. Another patient had been admitted while she'd been attending to Alice.

'Why were you so bothered about Di saying that she was going to report this business to the authorities on the mainland?' she asked as she bit into a large slice of moist gingerbread.

Tom swallowed an even larger mouthful. 'I wasn't,' he said. 'I'm not. I just didn't want to find it on Drummock.' His wide mouth quirked. 'I guess that I'm naïve, but I want this island to be perfect… I don't want anything ugly happening.' His eyes were sad as he spoke.

'Because of something that happened recently?'

'Yes. Not long before I left my London practice, my surgery was burgled and trashed and then the gang of hooligans came to my house and attempted to do the same. One of them had a gun, though he didn't use it. They broke windows, and had the police not arrived promptly, might well have done far worse.'

His eyes met Fee's. 'You can imagine how frightened the children were. From my point of view, it was the final straw at the end of a dreadful year.'

He stood up and walked toward the ward window, then smiled at her over his shoulder. 'Sorry about droning on about my problems.'

'Feel free any time,' said Fee. 'I'm glad that you've told me a little about yourself. It explains a great deal.' She touched his arm lightly. 'As I've told you before, the children will be safe here.'

'Yes, it's wonderful,' he replied. He nodded toward the ward. 'You've got another patient,' he said.

'Yes, Karen Strong. She's been sent back to recover from an appendicectomy performed a few days ago at St Cath's. I was called out to her one night and found her appendix on the point of rupturing—very nasty. She'd been boarding with Mrs Cox at the B&B.'

'Ah.' Tom grinned. 'Mrs Cox—my first patient, you might say.'

'Yes,' replied Fee rather curtly, not wanting to be reminded of that incident. 'The sad thing is, nobody knows much about Karen. She's English, but we're not sure if she's simply here on holiday or for some other reason, and she seems reluctant to say. We haven't pressed her because she's been so ill—still is, for that matter, which is why she's here. She's nowhere else to go to be looked after.'

'Do you want me to have a look at her?'

Did she want him to have a look at the new patient? There was a click as the kettle switched off. 'I'll make the tea,' she announced, moving swiftly into the kitchen.

If she asked the doctor to look at the patient, it really would seal him in his official capacity as medical officer to the hospital. Well, he is that anyway, she reminded herself. And by Monday, when he's working full time, young Karen Strong, like the other patients in the hospital and wherever they live on Drummock, *would* be his patient, not hers.

Except for the midwifery cases. They would still be more hers and Margot McBain's than his. She comforted herself with that thought. And, of course, she would still see plenty of patients needing dressings and injections and so forth, referred to her by the doctor.

Her stomach knotted up. This really was the moment that she had been dreading. The other people she had asked him to see had been emergencies. Karen wasn't an emergency. She had been admitted to the hospital to recuperate from surgery and be nursed back to health. Fee herself was perfectly capable of reading the report from St Cath's and examining her and assessing her needs. A week ago this was what she would have been doing.

Would have been—past tense!

She poured the tea, took it through to the office and placed a mug in front of him.

'Thank you, Doctor,' she said, pleased with the neutral tone of her voice. 'I would like you to check Karen out and write her up for whatever medication you think suitable.'

Tom looked at her steadily, his eyes thoughtful. He nodded toward the plate still loaded with gingerbread. 'May I?'

'Of course. Would you like something more substantial—bread and cheese or scrambled egg or something? I can get it from the main kitchen.'

What the devil am I doing, she wondered wryly as the words tumbled out of her mouth, playing the old-fashioned ward-sister bit, offering food to the poor, harassed, overworked doctor? This large, bronzed man who looks as if he's spent months in the sunshine isn't harassed or overworked—well, not yet he isn't. Although from what she'd just heard, he hadn't had such a trouble-free passage from London to Drummock.

Absent-mindedly, Fee took another piece of gingerbread and bit into it. But the winter was yet to come with the storms and accidents and some days being cut off from the mainland. She wondered if he'd last the course then. And out of the blue came the hope that he would. She frowned and shook her head. She didn't mean that, did she? She wanted him gone so that she could take the reins back into her own hands.

He shook his head. 'No, thanks, this is fine, very filling.'

What was he talking about? Oh, yes, the gingerbread.

'I can see the wheels churning,' he said softly. 'You know, we're both on the same side—the patients' side.'

How much had he divined of her mental ramblings?

'Yes, of course we are,' she said aloud. 'And talking of patients, what are we going to do about Alice?'

'I don't know,' he muttered, suddenly impatient and standing up to peer through the window into the ward again. 'Anywhere else, it would be simple. An undiagnosed patient, however ill, would be sent to the nearest hospital for investigation. But in her case...' He shrugged his wide shoulders so that the cotton of his shirt stretched. He turned to Fee, frowning. 'She's deteriorating rapidly. I'm doubtful whether she'd make the journey, poor old thing. Whichever way you look at it, this is Drummock and things are different here.'

So he'd learned that already.

Tom sat down again. 'Yet she might go on for days, perhaps weeks. If she were investigated and a firm diagnosis made, perhaps they could make her more comfortable than we can. They would be able to put her on powerful drugs and painkillers which, even if they were available here, I would hardly be justified in using without knowing exactly what is going on inside, would I?'

'Are you asking for my opinion?' Fee enquired, her sea-green eyes meeting his.

'Yes, please. What would you have done last week before I showed up?'

'What we're doing now, only I would have increased her painkillers because, even without a confirmed diagnosis, I would have suspected something sinister going on in her bowel and bladder. And I would have notified St Cath's, asked for a second opinion and stated that it was unlikely that Alice would survive the journey. Then I would have concentrated on making her comfortable for whatever time remained to her.'

He gave her a tight smile. 'You've got it all worked out, haven't you? Have you no doubts at all? No fears that you're perhaps making a mistake, especially in view of the fact that Miss McNabb is already gunning for us?'

Fee shook her head. 'No, and Di's not "gunning for us", as you put it. She simply wants to shake up the people who she feels are responsible for not supplying us with a doctor sooner and prevent such a thing happening again—perhaps to someone younger who would benefit from more intensive treatment than we can provide.'

Tom continued to eye her cautiously. 'Are you saying that she and the rest of the family will be satisfied that we can do as much for the old lady as necessary?' he asked.

'Yes, I think they will all want us to do exactly what I propose. Alice doesn't want to go anywhere. She's lived on Drummock all her life. She knows that she's dying and she wants to remain here with her friends and relatives. I think that we should respect her wishes.'

After a moment he said, 'All right, we'll do that. We'll do what we can for her with tons of TLC and hands-on nursing. As far as I'm concerned, that's the very best we can do for her, and to the devil with the consequences. Now, let's take a look at the new patient.'

Consequences, thought Fee. Will there be any for him? He was taking an unconventional step before he'd had time to get into his stride and prove that he's a good doctor. She had a moment of doubt. Should she have pushed him the way she had?

He moved across to the door and held it open. 'Lead the way, Miss McFie,' he said, bowing slightly.

A ripple of awareness shafted through her as she slid past him and caught a whiff of his clean male scent. Warning bells jangled in her head. Beware of his charm, they rang out loud and clear.

*   *   *

The meeting Fee had called for the following afternoon in the surgery waiting room for nursing and auxiliary staff to meet their new doctor was packed. Although several of them had now met Tom Cameron in connection with the emergencies that had arisen, there were still many who hadn't.

Everyone was there, from Joe Drummond, the ambulance-driver, to the cleaning ladies who kept the hospital and surgery spotless.

Tom paused in the doorway, looking a bit surprised by the number of people.

'Well, you did say everyone connected with the medical and nursing fraternity,' Fee reminded him as she met him at the door. 'And because there are so many part-timers and voluntary workers, that mounts up to quite a few. Some of them might not be needed for weeks, even months on end, but we do have our flu epidemics and other occasions when we're stretched, especially in the summer when there are a lot of holidaymakers.'

Tom widened his brilliant blue eyes and looked down at her. 'And you've been responsible for all this lot as well as your other duties, without medical back-up?'

Fee pulled a face and grinned wryly. 'Well, on paper a doctor was always on call from the mainland. I wasn't left entirely without support.'

'And in practice?'

'There was no one who felt responsible for Drummock. When I requested a doctor, a different one came each time. Early on, after the old doctor left, I suggested that someone hold a weekly surgery so that he or she could get to know the territory, but it never happened.'

'And everything was dumped on you?'

His sympathy for her was obvious but, having grumbled for months about lack of co-operation from the mainland, she suddenly found herself defending them. She and the inhabitants of Drummock might complain as much as they liked, but she couldn't allow this newcomer to criticise them without a challenge.

She replied in a sharp voice, 'You can't blame them really. Their resources are as stretched as everyone else's. We've got a brilliant helicopter service and the sound isn't very wide. Someone can get here quite fast if necessary.'

Tom smiled down at her. It was a lopsided, sardonic smile. A hank of fair hair, bleached fairer by the late sunshine, flopped over one eye. She had the uncomfortable feeling that he knew exactly why she was so sharp.

He murmured softly, 'But it's not for me to criticise, is it? I'm an outsider.'

Fee fought to keep the colour out of her cheeks. How should she answer him? It seemed churlish to agree with him after all the help he had given her, but he was still an outsider, someone who had turned up out of the blue and threatened to turn her life upside down. But although she felt threatened by him, not everyone felt the same. After all, he *was* a qualified doctor, as Alice had pointed out, and there was an air about him that was very reassuring. And, of course, he was loaded with charm. Half the women on the island, young or old, would fall for that.

Several people were beginning to look toward them, expecting them to move further into the room.

Fee decided to ignore the controversial question that he had left in the air.

'It's not quite as daunting as it perhaps looks,' she explained, going back to the comment that he had made earlier. 'I have terrific back-up from the senior nurses and people like Andrew Crawford—he's the local pharmacist. He's over there, the small chap with the red hair. He's a tower of strength. I'll introduce you in a minute.'

Tom accepted her change of tactics without comment.

'I see that you've laid on a buffet. It's more like a social get-together than the professional meeting that I envisaged. Or is that something that I shouldn't criticise either?'

So he had claws! He sounded as sharp as she had moments before.

'Some of these people,' she muttered through clenched teeth, 'have come straight from work, having missed lunch. Some of the young mothers have paid a childminder to cover for them. Some of the men are volunteers on the lifeboat and may get called out any time. And if you're worried about the cost coming out of the hospital budget, don't be. Friends of the hospital will pick up the tab.'

An extraordinary range of expressions flitted across his face—surprise, anger, humour, together with a touch of sadness. Finally humour surfaced uppermost.

He bent his head and whispered softly. 'I've a lot to learn haven't I? Please, don't write me off yet.'

The charm at work again. She met his stunning blue eyes, which were glinting with fun, and forced a smile as she suddenly remembered the advice she had given herself about at least appearing to present a friendly front to the world. And it was of paramount importance that their manner did nothing to fuel any feelings of animosity that anyone might be harbouring against the doctor simply because he was a newcomer.

Ian McKay already showed signs of disliking him simply because he saw him as a threat to Fee's authority—he had said as much to her and he hadn't even met the doctor yet. She gave herself a mental shake and said brightly, 'Come on, let's do the rounds. I'll hold your hand. We'll make for the buffet—there's nothing like a strong cuppa and a ham sandwich to set the ball rolling.'

Tom's eyes twinkled. 'Except the island's single malt with which to wet the baby's head. This is rather like a baptism, isn't it? Everyone's here to give me the once-over, just like one does with a new baby. I just hope that I pass the test.'

Fee said in surprise, 'You can't be nervous. After all, you insisted on meeting everyone. They're here at your bidding.'

'But I didn't think that it would be like this.' He looked round the crowded room.

'You thought that it would be more formal.'

'Yes.' He grinned ruefully. 'I expected everyone to be sitting in neat rows of chairs all facing the same way. And you would introduce me and I would explain briefly how I mean to run the practice. Then I would ask if anyone had any questions or suggestions and you would put names and jobs to faces. I thought that we might have a cup of tea then and shake hands with a few people, and that would be that.'

A wave of sympathy for him washed over Fee, and for the first time she looked from his point of view at what had happened since he'd arrived on Drummock. He was virtually a foreigner in a strange land. As far as she knew, he had lived and worked in England for many years in spite of his Scottish ancestry. He didn't appear to have any current Scottish connections, neither did he speak as if he had any close relatives or friends in England. In other words, he was on his own with his children. She really would have to make a huge effort to get along with him.

There was no question of protocol, Tom discovered as the afternoon drifted on. No one was singled out for special treatment. Fee introduced him to whoever they bumped into as they made their way to the buffet and then circulated with full plates, making casual contact with other people. One of the first, as promised, was Andrew Crawford.

'Nurse McFie and I have a well-established system for ordering and supplying drugs,' he announced firmly as soon as they had shaken hands, giving Tom a challenging look.

'Which I have no intention of changing,' replied Tom with equal firmness. 'Unless,' he added drily, 'I feel a real need to do so.'

'I see,' said Andrew simply.

I shouldn't have said that, thought Tom, but I'm damned if I'm going to be walked all over by small-town prejudice. Much as he needed to put down roots, he couldn't afford to do it by being a weak doctor. Patients wanted their doctor to be friendly but also strong and reassuring.

In their turn, the half-dozen or so other people whom he'd already met, such as the nurses and care assistants and cleaners from the hospital, came over to welcome him again.

Another person Tom recognised was James Forrester, whose wife Blanche had given birth to the bouncing baby Bruce. Surely he was the bank manager and not directly involved with the hospital?

'What's James Forrester doing here?' he asked Fee as

they watched him working his way through the throng toward them.

'He's the assistant chair of the hospital trustees,' she murmured just before James reached them.

James shook Tom's hand. 'I dare say you're surprised to see me,' he said.

'Fee has explained your role in relation to the hospital,' Tom replied. 'How many trustees are there?'

'Five,' replied James. 'Six with the chairman, Ian McKay, who has the casting vote. Like everything else on the island, we're a sort of miniaturised version of a larger hospital. The other trustees were unable to get here and send their apologies. We hope to arrange a formal meeting soon. I'm afraid that your early arrival, before we'd been informed of your appointment, rather threw us.'

'I'm sorry about that,' said Tom easily, without explaining that he'd been given the go-ahead from the mainland. 'And I'm sure that, although you're small, you're no less efficient than your larger counterparts. I'm much impressed by the day-to-day running of the hospital.'

James looked pleased, but said quickly, 'That's largely down to Fee, though obviously we give her our support. But I must thank you on behalf of the trustees for what you've done since you've arrived in Drummock,' he said. 'You were certainly thrown in at the deep end. We would have given you a proper welcome had we been informed earlier of your appointment.'

Tom waved the apology away. 'I'm just sorry that someone made a hash of everything.'

'I'd like to say that heads will roll, but I'm afraid we're only small fry as far as the mainland is concerned and we don't count for anything much.' James looked at his watch and offered his hand again. 'I must be off— my bread-and-butter job calls. I do wish you well on Drummock, Doctor. Anything that I can help you with, please, don't hesitate to ask.'

'Thank you. By the way, how's your wife and young Bruce?'

'Och, they're fine, thanks. Goodbye.'

Tom filed away the information that he'd just had from James Forrester and wondered how it had come about that even the trustees hadn't been notified of his appointment. The fact that the chairman, Ian McKay, had been away when he'd been appointed probably contributed to the mix-up. He hoped that was all it was, otherwise it almost smacked of a deliberate snub by the mainland authorities.

Fee continued to guide him round and introduce him to more people. A few names and faces stuck, but most were just a blur—he hoped he'd get to know them all eventually.

Late in the proceedings, a man wearing dirty jeans and a tweedy jacket that had seen better days entered the room. 'That's Ian McKay,' Fee explained, sounding apologetic. 'The chairman of the hospital management committee. He must have come straight off the farm and hasn't had time to tidy himself up, or he'd never have come in that state.'

Ian crossed the room to where Fee and Tom were standing and nodded at Tom.

'You must be Dr Cameron,' he said briskly. 'I won't shake hands—I've been manhandling a heifer that slipped in the slurry. Slurry has its own clinging qualities. I've showered, but you wouldn't know it. Not the best of introductions, I'm afraid, but welcome to

Drummock.' He produced a tight smile. 'I hope that you'll be able to give our Nurse McFie the support that she deserves. I'm afraid that I've got to shoot off again, but I'm sure that we'll bump into each other in the next few days.'

Tom's heart sank. What had he done to deserve such a cool welcome? He'd not even met the man before, and yet all the signals were that the hospital chairman wished Tom anywhere but on Drummock. It was almost as though he had taken against Tom personally.

When Ian had left, Fee said softly, 'I'm sure that Ian…' Her voice trailed off and she tried again. 'That Ian didn't mean to be so….'

'Rude!' exclaimed Tom. 'I'm afraid that he did. His attitude is the same as Joe Drummond's. Both men are very protective of you. With Joe being an elderly bachelor it's perhaps understandable, but McKay? I thought he was a happily married man whose wife has just given him another baby. Surely he's not—'

'How dare you,' cut in Fee fiercely, 'suggest any such thing? Ian and I were virtually brought up together, and when I returned to the island after my parents' accident, he supported me all the way. He's simply afraid that I'm going to be usurped.'

Tom nodded slightly. 'I stand corrected.'

She gave him a long, hard look. 'You've a lot to learn, Dr Cameron. No one else was rude to you as Ian was, but a lot of them have reservations about you being here. It'll take a long time to earn their respect and acceptance.'

She almost regretted having said it when she saw the expression on his face, but hardened her heart and remained cool as the room emptied.

Bell Hooper was the last to go. She didn't hide the

fact that she found Tom attractive. And he found her attractive, too. She was a tall woman with a good figure, strong, evenly featured face and a mass of dark hair unusual on Drummock. Probably in her late thirties, he guessed.

She was the hospital's physiotherapist, Fee had explained when she'd introduced her, though most of her work was done privately in the township. Not surprisingly, hers was one of the faces that had stuck.

'Dr Cameron,' she said as she was taking her leave, 'or may I call you Tom? It's more friendly.'

Tom grinned, finding her forthright manner refreshing after the blushes and stammers of some of the women he'd met that afternoon. 'Tom, please—definitely more friendly,' he agreed, thinking that he could do with all the friends he could muster after Fee's bombshell.

'I'd like to invite you to supper one evening,' she said, 'as a personal welcome to Drummock. Will you come?'

Tom bowed his head. 'How kind,' he said. 'I'd like that if I can persuade Maggie to childmind for me.'

Bell's well-marked eyebrows rose. 'Oh, I thought she was living in,' she said.

That's what comes of living in a fish bowl, thought Tom wryly. It works for and against. 'Well, we're still sorting things out,' he said cautiously, 'but if you ring me with a date, I'm sure that I can fix something.'

Her dark eyes lit up. 'Brilliant. I'll say goodbye, then. What an asset you're going to be to Drummock and to poor Fee. She's been run off her feet. Say goodbye to her for me. She seems to have disappeared.'

'Poor' Fee returned to the room as soon as Bell had gone, stifling her laughter.

Tom was pleased to see her smiling, even though it

was at his expense. He said severely, 'So what happened to you, deserting me in my hour of need?'

Fee tried to look innocent. 'I found a stray plate that had been overlooked and returned it to the kitchen. Anyway, I thought that you were having a private conversation.'

Her eyes teased him and her mouth was tilted up at the corners. Fee was a beautiful woman, too, though as unlike Bell Hooper as it was possible to be, with her cloud of fair hair and slender figure. Tom felt his spirits soar. At this moment and for however brief a time, they were enjoying a joke together and it felt good.

He stared down at her for a moment, fascinated and unable to move. If only it could always be like this between them. It should be for, as he'd pointed out, they were both on the patients' side.

Fee blinked to cut eye contact and led the way to the door. 'I'd better lock up,' she said, and there was a husky tremor in her voice. 'There's no evening surgery. The next surgery is tomorrow morning, just a short one from eight to ten as it's Saturday.' They were by now outside the door and she was turning the key in the lock.

'Do you think I might sit in?' asked Tom, 'so that I get the feel of it.'

'Good idea. In fact, I was going to suggest that if you can spare the time and sort out Simeon and Philly, we should spend the morning going through the routine— looking at notes and the ordering system for drugs and equipment and discussing the various clinics that we run, and so on. And we must sort out keys—there are dozens of them.'

It was the first time she had spoken of the children by name, he noted, surprised by how much it pleased him. He felt—hoped—that it was another step toward being accepted. And he badly needed to belong to this tight community, both for his own sake and the children's, and for that he needed Fee's support—if he still had it after his encounter with Ian McKay.

Watching his face, Fee said, 'Now I can see *your* wheels turning, but I can't make out if you think a Saturday run-through would be a good thing.'

He smiled and set her mind at rest. 'I think it's your best idea yet,' he said. 'I can't wait to get cracking.'

CHAPTER EIGHT

IT WAS Saturday morning and Fee woke feeling ragged after a restless night. She had been disturbed by strange dreams that had flitted in and out of her consciousness. They had one thing in common, though—they were all associated with Tom.

Her heartbeats quickened at the thought that she would be seeing him later when they shared the morning surgery...

'*Oh, come on!*' she exclaimed loudly, and leapt out of bed and across to the window which had been open all night to the balmy October air. Anybody would think she was starting to fancy the man!

That was just the sort of foolish thought his type inspired, that was all. The sort of thing women joked about between themselves. But it was serious; it wasn't actually genuine love...

Love!

Now she'd admitted the word to herself even as she wondered at the absurdity of it. No way was she in love with Dr Cameron, or ever likely to be. It was an extraordinary and ridiculous idea. She didn't even like Tom Cameron very much...did she?

Yes, she did, she realised belatedly the moment she saw him enter the surgery shortly after she did. The pulses in her throat beat uncomfortably fast, and her breath came in shallow, uneven inspirations.

No, it couldn't be happening to her. Not out of the

blue like this. It was a cliché. She had expected that half the women of Drummock would fall under his spell. After all, he was what the older women called a fine figure of a man and the younger ones called a hunk. But she wasn't looking for a man. She was independent, she had her work, her lovely house and a host of friends.

In the moments that it took Tom to cross from the door to the desk, Fee mentally listed the whole catalogue of reasons proving Tom Cameron was of no personal interest to her. The trouble was, she wasn't sure she believed them.

'Good morning,' he said, smiling widely, showing his even white teeth. He rubbed his hands together. 'Touch of autumn in the air at last, I think.'

'Yes,' Fee replied breathily. 'The weather seems to be on the turn at last. Please, do sit down.' She patted the chair beside her at the desk. How silly and stilted she sounded.

His hand brushed hers as he sat down and she had difficulty stopping herself shivering with pleasure. How could things have changed overnight? Why, oh, why was she suddenly so aware of him? Had it something to do with yesterday when she'd suddenly become conscious that he was on his own? It had been an eye-opener to see him there on her territory, the only stranger amongst a crowd of people whom she'd known for ever. How vulnerable he'd looked.

Her heart turned over. She'd wanted to reach out and touch him, reassure him. She wanted to reach out and touch him now, sitting inches away from her, the warmth from his body an invitation.

She took a deep breath and glanced sideways at him. He was watching her and their eyes met for an instant. His, she saw with surprise, were full of tenderness.

'What's wrong, Fee?' he asked softly. 'You're all prickly and on edge.'

'Nothing,' she replied untruthfully, and then more honestly added, 'Nothing you can do anything about.'

'Try me.' He looked hopefully at her and for one moment she was on the point of spilling out her muddled thoughts. Fortunately common sense came to her rescue and she shook her head decisively.

'We'd better get on. No idea how many patients will turn up on a Saturday morning. It's treated as an emergency clinic and varies considerably, according to the weather and how many holidaymakers there are around. Because it's been so fine over the last few weeks there are more people still on holiday than usual.'

Briefly she thought that Tom was going to persist in his questioning, but he didn't and to Fee's relief the conversation became patient-orientated. 'What sort of things do patients usually present with?' he asked after a moment.

'Well, in high summer it's mainly heat rash, sunburn and too much rich food and drink. At the moment it's likely to be windburn. People don't realise the power of salt spray and wind when the sun gets a bit lower in the sky. And too much rich food, especially shellfish. There are some good catches coming in at present—the lobsters are especially fine and visitors appreciate the freshness. But some of them aren't used to the quantity and richness.'

'Amen to that,' said Tom feelingly. 'Maggie cooked me lobster last night for my dinner, after the children had gone to bed full of home-made fish cakes and chips. I must say that the quality and freshness of the food and Maggie's super cooking are bonuses to living on Drummock that have completely taken me by surprise.'

The mention of Maggie reminded Fee that she had a bone to pick with that lady. What had she meant by leading Tom to believe that she'd made derogatory remarks about Simeon and Philly? The sooner that matter was put right, the better.

'It must be lonely for you,' she said, 'after the children have gone to bed.'

Now, why on earth had she said that? It annoyed her that she felt somehow responsible for his loneliness. What on earth did it matter to her that he was lonely? After all, she lived on her own and she didn't feel lonely.

'Used to be in London,' he replied tersely, 'but not here.'

'Oh, good,' she murmured rather feebly as Kirsty, the nurse on duty, came in with a pile of patient notes.

Tom picked up the top folder from the small pile.

'"Farley McKay",' he read out aloud. 'Presumably a relation of Ian's?'

Fee frowned. 'The eldest of Ian's brothers, It's not like Farley to show up on a Saturday morning, so it won't be anything trivial.' She disappeared into the examination cubicle with a roll of paper towelling.

Farley entered the office a few moments later.

He was obviously a good deal older than Ian, with greying hair and piercing grey eyes. His face was drawn and lined and it was clear that he was in pain.

He halted just inside the door, his eyes resting on Tom. The expression in them was hostile. He began to back out.

'Sorry,' he muttered. 'Thought that Fee was taking surgery.'

'She is. I'm assisting, getting to know the ropes, as it were,' said Tom, standing up and offering his hand. 'I know your brother Ian slightly.'

Farley nodded, but didn't shake hands.

Fee came out from behind the curtains round the examination couch.

'Morning, Farley. Sit yourself down. Now, what can we do for you? Wrists bothering you again?'

'Not excessively,' Farley replied, perching himself on the edge of the seat. 'But I'm feeling the strain a bit. Could you up the ibuprofen? I've got some work that I must finish by the end of next week. Something of a deadline situation.'

Tom was looking through Farley's records on the monitor. 'But you're on the maximum dose now, Mr McKay, and you've been on it for a long time. Perhaps a change of anti-inflammatories would be beneficial?'

Farley glared at him and then turned to Fee. 'What do you think, Miss McFie?' he said, as if Tom wasn't there.

Fee thought faster than she ever had before. She couldn't let Farley McKay treat the doctor like that, but no way could she let Farley down and flatly ignore his request. In spite of what he'd said about managing the pain, she was sure that he was in considerable distress.

She felt Tom tense beside her and prayed that he wouldn't erupt. He had every right to do so. What the devil had got into Farley? It wasn't like him to be rude, unless he was following Ian's lead which was based on his personal feelings of antipathy toward Tom because of his misplaced protectiveness of herself.

Farley stood up. 'It doesn't matter,' he said. 'Shouldn't have put you in this position, Fee. I'll manage.'

Tom stood up, too. 'Mr McKay,' he said softly, 'I'm sorry. Fee knows you better than I do and can assess what you need better than I can. I see by your notes that you're an architect, so the severe arthritis in your wrists must be particularly restricting and sometimes interfere with your work. You obviously do need a great deal of pain relief. Suppose we put our heads together and sort something out for you—at least as a temporary measure while you complete this project. Would that help?'

Fee applauded him silently. It was a neat suggestion and beautifully put.

Farley stared at him and then sat down heavily. 'Can you do something about these?' he said, painfully shrugging his hands from the sleeves of his jacket.

Very gently, Tom took the bony hands in his. They were thin, slender even, except around the finger and wrist joints. They were artist's hands. Tom examined them carefully, lightly smoothing his fingers over the swollen areas.

'Yes,' he said quietly, 'I can do something about it, especially as a short-term emergency measure. And I think that Miss McFie will approve of it.' He glanced at Fee. 'I dare say she would have suggested something similar. There are treatments with cortisone drugs that I think we might try, especially short term, and some anti-inflammatory, which I see you have had before. Did you stop it because you had side effects with that?'

'No, I had a bad dose of flu and bronchitis and Fee thought I'd better come off it temporarily. And then my joints improved slightly and there was no point in going back on it. I'm afraid that I get a bit impatient with medication and sometimes feel that I want to throw the lot in. But usually Fee persuades me to stick with it.'

They both looked at Fee. Farley's eyes were full of admiration…and something more. He's in love with her, thought Tom. Fee's cheeks turned pink beneath her golden tan under their joint scrutiny.

She said quickly, staring at the monitor, 'I think it was the antibiotics and the weather being so warm and dry that did the trick on that occasion. Now I think antibiotics plus a short course of cortisone and a painkilling injection daily for the next week should see you through, Farley, if Dr Cameron agrees.'

'Absolutely,' said Tom. 'I was thinking of something along those lines. How do you feel about that, Mr McKay?' he asked Farley.

'Anything,' replied the architect, 'if I can just get on with my work.'

'And afterwards will you come and have another chat with me, and Fee if she can spare the time, so that we can work out a plan for both wrists? They need to be splinted and properly rested for a while and then be given gentle physio. Hopefully that will set you up for the winter.'

Farley's bushy eyebrows rose and his eyes opened wide. 'Do you mean physio from Bell Hooper?' he asked, his voice full of trepidation. 'The merry divorcee? She scares me stiff.'

'Well, of course Bell,' said Fee, her eyes twinkling.

Tom chuckled. 'Strictly between ourselves, she scares me, too, and I've only met her the once,' he admitted, in a carefully judged show of candour. 'But I bet she's a damned good physio.'

He and Farley exchanged man-to-man looks of understanding. Fee hid a smile and began to set up syringes for the injections.

A little later Farley was ready to leave. He already looked a little more relaxed as the painkilling drug began to take effect. At the door he paused and nodded toward Tom. 'Welcome to Drummock, Dr Cameron,' he said.

'Fee needs all the help—medical help, I mean—that she can get. She's been coping on her own for far too long.'

It was a polite, reconciliatory speech, almost an apology for his earlier rudeness, and yet...

Tom and Fee looked at each other after Farley had gone. They knew without exchanging a word that there was an underlying message in the speech. The emphasis on the word 'medical' had clearly defined certain boundaries.

'I think,' said Tom drily, 'that I'm being warned off anything other than a strictly professional friendship.' His eyes gleamed. 'You seem to have a string of protectors on Drummock, Miss McFie. I'd better watch my step.'

'Do them good to have a bit of competition,' Fee replied with a chuckle. Hot on the heels of those words came the embarrassing realisation of what her remark had implied. 'We'd better get on,' she said briskly. 'We've a lot to do this morning.'

They found plenty to do all day. At one o'clock Tom suggested that they go out to lunch. 'My treat,' he said, 'if you come up with a restaurant.'

'The Gull, just off Quay Point,' she said. 'Marvellous views all round, but we'd better check that they've got a table. A coach party came off the ferry earlier and they may have filled the place. It's great in the winter with no visitors about—it's like being on a floating island high above the sea.'

Tom looked into her shining eyes and marvelled that a woman so attractive, clever and intelligent and with so much warmth about her should still be unmarried and apparently contented. What a wonderful wife and mother she would make some lucky guy... What a wonderful

wife and mother she would make for me and the children, came the sudden staggering thought. His heart
seemed to turn over and his pulse accelerated.

Don't be ridiculous, man, he told himself sharply.
What woman in her right mind would want to take on
a thirty-eight-year-old man with a load of unsavoury
baggage and two lively kids? Besides, half the time she
seems to resent me. And for that matter, she's not the
easiest person to get on with. So why am I feeling this
way about her? He firmly stopped his train of thought.

'I'll ring and find out,' he said, pulling the local di-
rectory toward himself and reaching for the phone.

The restaurant was all that Fee had said. There definitely
was a sensation of floating, similar to that of the captain's home in The Crow's Nest at the other end of the
island.

'This is fantastic,' remarked Tom as they sat down at
a table by the window shaped like the prow of a sailing
ship. The sun warmed them even as it glinted on the
smooth sea swirling below them.

Fee said, 'It is, isn't it?' She gestured to include the
wide view over the Atlantic to the west, and then the
sound and the distant mainland just visible through a
light haze.

Tom grinned, his eyes drinking in her lovely animated
face. 'You love Drummock, don't you? You always
speak of it as if it belongs to you.'

'Well, in a way it does,' came her surprising reply.
'My family were the first to settle on the island centuries
ago when it was inhabited only by a few sheep and occasional visiting pirates, marauders—call them what you
will. Then the McFies were on the wrong side during
the Rebellion and got separated from the main body of

those fleeing from the enemy in a thick fog. They were further up the coast and making for Skye.'

Slowly Tom lowered the menu he had just picked up. 'Are we talking Bonny Prince Charlie and all that?' he asked incredulously.

Fee nodded. 'Yep! Our lot supported him.'

'Well, I'm damned,' said Tom. 'I feel as if I'm in the presence of royalty.'

'Far from being royal stock...' Fee chuckled '...one of my ancestors was a swashbuckling pirate. He had his way with one of the McFie women amongst those first settlers. In those days, of course, with only sailing ships and rowing boats available, the island must have seemed a long way from the mainland. I imagine it was pretty wild and there were no laws or any sort of protection. The McFie clan were very much on their own.'

'Better and better,' said Tom. 'What a history—makes mine seem very tame. Well, most of it is tame.'

'Most of it? What about the bit that isn't?'

'Can't compare with yours.' An expression of pain flickered across his face. He picked up the menu again. 'I think we should order,' he said quickly.

They were both hungry after their busy morning and chose thick vegetable soup laced with sherry for starters. In spite of the continuing October sunshine, there was a decided nip in the air. It really did look as if summer was at last on the wane.

'This is very good,' said Tom, tearing off a chunk of warm bread roll. 'Almost a meal in itself.'

'Drummock women are famous for their soups,' said Fee. 'We use lots of wild herbs, both in medicine and in food. Probably necessary a few hundred years ago when there wasn't much meat around and what there was was pretty tough and inedible. Of course, fish was the main source of protein.'

'You must have missed the island when you went away to do your training,' hazarded Tom.

'I did. I almost didn't go, but all I ever wanted to do was nursing. And I wanted the best, and Edinburgh offered it. I was able to switch from course to course and end with a special degree course they were running.'

'So what brought you back to Drummock when you could have got a prestigious hospital job anywhere in the world with your qualifications?'

Fee contemplated the spoonful of soup midway between her bowl and her mouth, and a look of such anguish passed over her face that Tom wished that he hadn't asked the question. A broken love affair perhaps?

'My parents were both drowned in a sailing accident not far from the shore. The weather suddenly changed, as it can in these waters—a fact that I'm always reminding visitors about. They were both first-class sailors and were making for port. Only they never made it. I came home for the funeral and to sort things out with my brothers. They're scattered all over the place.'

'How many brothers have you got?'

'Three. Jamie and Robbie are twins. They're thirty-one—a couple of years older than me. They're in the States, although they're far apart and don't see much of each other. Fergus is twenty-seven and farms in Australia. We all get together around Christmas and New Year. It may sound funny to say that we are a close-knit family, scattered as we are, but it's true.'

'But why did you stay once you'd settled your parents' affairs? You must have been holding down a good job.'

'I was, but I couldn't bear the thought that there

wouldn't be anybody representing our branch of the clan if I left. None of my brothers could stay, so it was up to me. Sentimental rubbish, of course, but there you go.'

The waiter cleared their soup bowls then brought their main course.

Then Tom said. 'I thought that there were loads of McFies on Drummock.'

'There are, but none directly descended from the original family who started the settlement. It didn't seem right somehow to leave the family home empty.'

He frowned. 'And you gave up your career for…?'

'An ideal, pie-in-the-sky.' Fee shrugged. 'And I've never regretted it. And the gods were with me. Shortly after I made my decision, the district nurse retired and I took her place. The rest you know. Old Dr Franks was clinging on but getting frail. There were problems getting another doctor until you turned up, so my extra qualifications came into their own.'

'No wonder I'm not exactly flavour of the month with some of the islanders…or with you,' he added drily.

'It doesn't matter,' said Fee, 'as long as we make it work. And talking of work, I think the best thing we can do to round off the day is to check the visits you'll have to do on Monday and work out the best route for you to take. Or would you like me to do them while you concentrate on the surgery and hospital?'

Tom shook his head. 'No, thanks. I've got to work on my own at some point. Monday will be as good a time as any. But I would like to know if there will be a nurse on call to do dressings, and so on.'

'Yes, Jeanie Beech. You met her at the party.'

'In her twenties, fair hair like yours, bubbly personality.'

'You have an eye for a pretty girl.' Fee laughed. 'Her

fiancé is a pilot with the helicopter service. Big chap who's used to heaving stretchers on and off the chopper. They're to be married in the spring.'

'You might say that she's spoken for, then,' said Tom, also laughing.

'You might say that,' said Fee.

It was one of those happy moments when everything gelled perfectly and there was a flow of understanding between them. Their eyes met and held again as they had earlier in the day. If only it could be like this all the time, thought Fee, but knew that it wouldn't be. Life wasn't like that.

It would be a long time before all the islanders accepted Tom, and people like Ian McKay and the pharmacist and others wanted Fee all to themselves, wanted her to go on reigning supreme. It could only happen on a place like Drummock with its close community linked by a wild and romantic history.

They called in at the hospital on their way back to the surgery to check on their patients there.

Jane was in the office. 'We've just admitted Jack Robinson,' she said.

'Jack is usually the first of our winter regulars,' Fee explained to Tom. 'He farms a few sheep and lives on his own. Bitter experience has taught us that if we have him in, feed him and boost him up with antibiotics at the first sign of bronchitis, we can get on top of it for the winter.'

'But who admitted him?' asked Tom. 'We were at lunch. Did he just walk in and admit himself?'

'Something like that. He knows the drill and so do the staff.' She turned to the staff nurse. 'Who brought Jack in, Jane?' she asked.

'The postie. He thought Jack looked pretty groggy and

didn't have to do much persuading to get him to come. I've given him the once-over. His lung bases sound grim and he's running a bit of a temperature. In other words, it's the usual picture.'

Tom raised his eyebrows and looked bewildered. Would he ever get used to these parochial ways of doing things? Everything was so casual. Nobody stood on ceremony. In London it took heaven knew how many phone calls to a whole list of hospitals and much pleading with bed managers to get someone admitted.

Yet here on Drummock a staff nurse could make a decision to admit someone as a prophylactic measure, and make a preliminary examination.

Fee was reading his mind. 'It's called cutting through the red tape,' she murmured with a smile. 'Possibly it can only work in a small community.'

'But what happens if you have a flu epidemic or an accident involving a number of people who have to be hospitalised? Even waiting for them to be transferred to the mainland must take time when you need beds.'

'We put up more beds in the ward, and if that gets full we use the waiting area. Three years ago we filled up with early flu victims and a number of visitors— ornithologists who came to watch some rare birds on their migration. Unfortunately the bird watchers brought salmonella with them, picked up from a hotel they'd stayed in.'

Tom said wryly, 'I can't wait to hear how you solved that one.'

Fee grinned. 'While the authorities were debating what to do about it, we opened up the school as an annexe to the hospital and staffed it with a couple of qualified nurses, assisted by a band of volunteers. It was all over in a few days. No one was the worse for the disruption and we didn't have a single fatality.'

'I think,' said Tom, digesting this information, 'that I'd better have a look at the new admission. Will you please lead the way, Staff Nurse?'

'My pleasure,' said Jane, twinkling up at him.

They're going down like ninepins, thought Fee with a mental shrug. Well, that's all right with me as long as he doesn't get big-headed and try using his followers to bring in too many innovations. At least until he knows what he is talking about.

But it wasn't all right with her, she realised as she watched Tom and Jane walk together down the ward. She almost resented her friend walking side by side with him.

She stayed in the office for fifteen minutes and caught up with some paperwork and made a couple of phone calls. Looking through the ward window, she saw that Tom was perched on the side of the captain's bed. He was having a three-way conversation of sorts with the captain, Mrs Mack and Jane.

This is where I bow out, Fee thought. It's his responsibility now. A cold hand seemed to clutch at her heart and squeeze it. It was the end of an era. She let herself quietly out of the office.

That evening, Fee walked up the quay toward the home where she'd been born and had lived most of her life. Her mind was brimming with confused thoughts. Above her the sky was full of stars and a young moon was rising. She took a deep breath of clear air, and smiled ruefully.

'Whatever comes, I could never,' she murmured to herself, 'live anywhere else but on Drummock.'

CHAPTER NINE

FEE'S phone rang at five-thirty the next morning. She stretched and wallowed for a few seconds before picking up the receiver. A few weeks ago there would have been a glimmer of dawn light even this early, but this morning it was still pitch dark. It never failed to surprise her how quickly the nights lengthened once they got toward the end of October.

'Hello, Fee,' said the voice on the other end. 'It's Jimmy McCallister here. I think Stella's started having contractions. Well, something's happening and you said to let you know if things looked as if they were moving, because of her blood pressure.'

'That's right, Jimmy. How does she seem?'

'Fine. I'm the one who's tearing my hair out.'

'Good job you've got plenty of it, then, isn't it?' Fee teased. 'Make a nice pot of tea. I'll be over in about half an hour.'

She thought about the young couple as she showered and dressed and nibbled some toast. They were both in their early twenties and had recently returned to Drummock specifically to have their baby on the island.

They were teachers, and until a short while ago had worked in Aberdeen on the east coast. Now Jimmy was teaching in Skleet across the sound and Stella was taking maternity leave. Apart from her high blood pressure, she was having a trouble-free pregnancy.

Fee frowned as she drove over to the McCallisters' bungalow on the outskirts of the town. It was a bit of a mystery as to why Stella's blood pressure was so high, although it occasionally went down a little. In every other respect she was fit and healthy, as one would expect of a physical training teacher. All the tests she'd had before and since she'd moved back to Drummock had been textbook perfect.

Even at St Cath's, where Fee had sent her for a check-up with the consultant obstetrician, they hadn't found anything else wrong and had confessed that there didn't seem to be a reason for the swinging blood pressure. Professor Black, the obstetrician, hadn't objected to Stella returning to Drummock, although she'd asked Fee to call her in if there were any problems.

'This young woman,' she'd told Fee on the phone, 'is as fit as the proverbial flea. She's not even complaining of headaches. I've never come across anything like it personally and I've been doing this job for thirty years, though I do vaguely remember reading of a like case in the *Lancet* years ago. Of course, people can walk round with high blood pressure and not know that they have it, but it's a very rare phenomenon in pregnancy for it not to produce side effects. Where blood pressure is high, there are normally any number of symptoms, from headaches, faintness, sickness to a poorly developing foetus. But with your Mrs McCallister, nothing.'

And Margot McBain, who had been delivering babies for more than thirty years, couldn't recall a similar case either.

'But, then, everything about babies is a mystery,' she'd said. 'No two pregnancies or deliveries are alike. Let's just play it as it comes, Fee, as long as young Stella and her husband are fully in the picture. I think though that we should work together on this one right from the off. We should relieve each other so that one of us is with her all the time once contractions start. If anything's going to go wrong, that's when it's likely to be.'

For the last week Stella had been under instructions to rest as much as possible, and Fee or Margot had visited twice every day. Over the last couple of days Stella's blood pressure had gone down a little, which was encouraging.

When Fee arrived at the McCallister residence she immediately took Stella's blood pressure, and found that it had fallen yet again. It was still high by normal standards, but nothing like it had been. She entered it on the chart that she and Margot had been using over the week and which was full of peaks and troughs.

'We'll be recording it half-hourly until your waters break and the contractions properly get going,' she informed Stella, 'and then we'll take it quarter-hourly. Now, I'll check you and the baby and see where we are at.'

'You're both fine,' Fee said a little while later, patting Stella's bump. 'Baby's heartbeat is strong and is quite unstressed. Now, Jimmy, how's that tea doing?'

'Stewing nicely,' said a relieved Jimmy, giving his wife's hand a squeeze before making for the door.

'I'll be back in a minute,' Fee told Stella, following Jimmy out. In the kitchen she leaned against the sink and watched as he poured the tea. 'You're more worried than you're letting on, aren't you, Jimmy?'

He nodded. 'Aye. Stella's so unconcerned in spite of the high blood pressure, yet she's always been hot on blood pressure. Teaching sport as she does, it's important to her. She normally does a lot of swimming and has been swimming daily until a few weeks ago. She was allowed to use the pool at school after hours. And I know that she believes that swimming is one of the best ways of keeping down blood pressure and generally keeping fit.'

'I wish we'd known earlier,' said Fee. 'The fact that she's suddenly stopped swimming may have some bearing on her pressure building up, though I can't quite see the connection. Had I known it was part of her regime, I could have arranged for her to go to St Cath's daily to use their physio pool.'

Jimmy pushed a mug toward her. He looked apologetic. 'Sorry, Fee, that's why Stella didn't tell you. She was afraid that if she started attending they would try to persuade her to have the baby in St Cath's, and we both want the baby to be born on Drummock. That's why we've come back from Aberdeen, but—'

Fee butted in, 'If there's any danger to Stella or the baby, you want her to go to St Cath's where they've got all the mod cons, right?'

'Right,' responded Jimmy. He laid his hand on Fee's arm. 'Even if she doesn't want to go, you must persuade her. I'm as much a traditionalist as she is, but not if it puts her or the baby at risk.'

'Point taken. Very sensible,' replied Fee. 'There's no way that either Margot or I would allow her to stay if we thought that she should be in hospital, and I'm sure that she's sensible enough to agree to go in if there's any danger to her or the baby. But we should trust her instincts at this moment. Mums-to-be often have a clear perception of their own needs. And she really is so well in every respect. Now, take your tea in and have it with her while I make a couple of phone calls. And try not to let your anxiety show.'

The morning and early afternoon passed without incident. Stella's blood pressure remained stable at the ele-

vated but not too frightening a level it had reached earlier. Fee phoned St Cath's and left a message for
Professor Black, updating her on Stella's progress.

Margot, when she arrived to take over from Fee, expressed her satisfaction with Stella's condition. 'Your
contractions are coming along nicely lass. Slow and far
apart as yet, but once your waters have broken we'll be
on course for a straightforward delivery.'

Fee welcomed Margot's calm and common sense, but
murmured to herself as she drove home, 'Keep your fingers crossed.' Margot had expressed similar sentiments
over the Forrester baby after it had been turned, and
she'd been right. But it was a bit much to expect two
miracles in a short space of time.

She was nearly back at her flat when she passed the
Cameron family walking up from the quay. They drew
level with her as she pulled up in front of her house and
climbed out, pulling her midwifery bag after her.

'Busy?' Tom asked, his eyes on the bag.

The handle of the bag seemed to burn through Fee's
fingers. Dear Lord, she'd forgotten Tom. Should she, out
of courtesy, have informed him when Stella's contractions had first started? It had been so long since she'd
been responsible to a third party, especially in the midwifery field, that the idea of involving anyone else simply hadn't occurred to her. And after all, though Stella
was a resident on the island, she was still under the care
of Professor Black. Surely that satisfied protocol?

But looking at Tom's face, she knew that the explanation was going to go down like a lead balloon. Oh,
why had the man come to Drummock and upset her busy
but contented existence?

She played for time. 'Busy? Yes you could say that,'

she replied, with a smile for the children. 'Been doing anything interesting?' she asked them.

'Helping Sam—he's Maggie's brother—scrape barnacles off the bottom of his rowing boat,' explained Philly, holding out small, grubby, scratched hands for Fee to inspect.

'Not his big boat,' Simeon told her seriously, 'but his little one that he uses when he goes fishing. We're going to help him paint the boat when it's dried out. It hasn't got a name like the big one has. That's called *Isle of Skye*. Sam says that we can choose a name for the little one if we'd like to. Dad says that we should make a list and—'

'I think,' Tom interrupted him firmly, 'that Miss McFie has heard enough about the boat. She's probably been up since the crack of dawn and wants to get home.'

He smiled down at his son, but when he lifted his head to look at Fee there was no trace of a smile.

Time to mend bridges yet again, thought Fee, squashing her irritation. Why did he always make her seem at fault? Surely she wasn't always in the wrong.

'Look, why don't you come up to the flat and have...' She checked her watch—half past three. Time had flown by at the McCallisters'. She and Jimmy had had a sandwich lunch and soon after that Margot had arrived to relieve her. 'An early tea,' she suggested.

She could see that Tom meant to refuse, and added quickly, 'I can give you the details on this case.' She looked suggestively at her delivery bag.

'Oh, please, Daddy, let's go to tea with Fee,' pleaded Philly.

Simeon was frowning and looking uncertain, as if he'd caught his father's reluctance.

'There's a special chute running from the top of the

house down to the garden,' Fee said quickly. 'It was for goods waiting to be loaded on board the merchant ships in the harbour. That was when the house was first built and my family owned cargo boats.' She didn't say at that point that it was probably used for smuggled goods, too—and, for that matter, people to be hauled up and hidden in the attic.

Simeon's eyes lit up. 'It really goes all the way down to the garden?'

Fee nodded. Simeon turned to his father.

'Dad, let's stay and have tea with Nurse McFie.'

Bright kid, thought Fee. 'Nurse McFie' showed a token sort of reserve. He's going to be as clever as his father one day.

Tom looked at the pleading faces of his offspring and predictably gave in. '*That*,' he said in a low voice, 'was below the belt.'

Fee couldn't tell if he was teasing or serious.

'I didn't mean to do that,' she said, and then added truthfully, 'Although I hoped it would be an incentive. And it will give us an opportunity to talk.'

'I mean to keep you to that,' he said, his voice hard. 'We damn well need to.'

'Fair enough,' said Fee. 'Now, shall we go up?'

She led the way up the winding iron staircase, the children hot on her heels and Tom bringing up the rear.

Philly and Simeon exclaimed over the fascinating long narrow kitchen, with its nooks and crannies and recesses and huge window at the end looking out across fields toward Ben Drummock in the distance.

'Wow!' exclaimed Simeon. Then, frowning and looking amazingly like his father, he turned to Fee. 'But I don't see the chute.'

'Unlock that door beside you,' replied Fee, pointing

to a massive key hanging on the wall. 'Only be careful because there's a floor-to-ceiling opening in the outside wall.'

Tom barked out, 'Wait Simeon.' Sliding past Fee and Philly, he unhooked the key before the boy had moved. 'You wait there, Philly,' he said over his shoulder as he put the key in the lock.

Philly slipped her hand into Fee's and smiled up at her. 'Daddy's always afraid that we're going to get hurt,' she explained earnestly. 'It's ever since...' She stopped and chewed at her lip, and finally murmured, 'Daddy says that it's better not to talk about it to strangers.'

Fee longed to deny that she was a stranger and encourage Philly to reveal more about the Cameron family and the mystery surrounding them, but knew that it wouldn't be true. As yet she *was* still a stranger and she sensed that, of all people, Tom wouldn't want her to be privy to family secrets.

'I'm sure Daddy's quite right,' she said. 'But I hope that one day we'll grow to be friends and not strangers.'

'Oh, so do I,' said Philly. She let go of Fee's hand and pirouetted along the polished boards toward the window. 'Look, I'm a ballet dancer,' she bubbled, curving her arms gracefully above her head.

'Is that what you want to be?' asked Fee.

'Oh, yes,' breathed Philly. 'Or some sort of dancer, anyway.'

Simeon stuck his head round the side door to the chute.

'Come on, Philly,' he called. 'It's brilliant! It's like a giant slide at the fair. There's a huge hook on a chain that was used to swing heavy stuff into the chute and at the bottom you can hook up anything from the ground.'

His sister gave a very adult feminine shrug. 'We'd better go and look,' she said indulgently.

'You go,' suggested Fee. 'I'm going to start getting the tea ready.'

'OK,' replied the little girl, dancing her way to the door.

Quickly Fee rustled up the sort of tea she thought the children would like, and then called them to the table. They'd been out in the fresh air and, whatever they'd eaten during the afternoon, she was sure that they would be starving.

They were. With strict instructions that they weren't to go into the loft room next door, she and Tom moved to the sitting room with a pot of tea and a fruit cake leaving the children to make short work of sausages, chips and beans and a stack of bread and butter with a selection of jams.

'You may have the TV on if you like,' Fee said as she and Tom left the room, 'if your father doesn't mind you watching whilst you're eating.'

Tom shook his head. 'Special occasion,' he murmured.

'That was delicious,' said Tom demolishing the last of the huge slice of cake Fee had placed on his plate. He wiped crumbs from his mouth with a paper napkin. 'Your creation?'

'No, my tenant in the flat below. A lovely old lady who spoils me rotten. She meets me with a wee dram and a bowl of stew on cold winter's nights.'

He gave her a quizzical look, and his face, which had been stern, seemed to soften. 'I'm glad that you've got someone looking out for you,' he said, with evident sincerity.

For some reason it made her uneasy that this man who hadn't as yet a friend on the island should be concerned about her. She took a deep breath and said huskily, 'Don't you want to know about the maternity case I've just come from?'

'Of course. Tell me,' he said.

It didn't take long to fill him in on Stella's background and suddenly it seemed ridiculous to think that she had kept back the information. Why had she? She could easily have phoned him earlier and put him in the picture.

Medical correctness didn't come into it. It was simply a question of politeness. But she simply hadn't thought of him in spite of the bewildering warm and emotional feelings that had assailed her yesterday. It was as if he didn't exist—and that was a horrible thought, and palpably untrue since there he was sitting opposite her, large and unruffled.

She felt herself blushing furiously. She got up from the table and crossed to the window. The sitting room was at the front of the house and looked down over the quay. The late afternoon ferry was coming in and Fee recognised many of the people getting off the boat in the twilight. It underlined the fact that her roots were here on Drummock whilst Tom's were...where? She turned and stared thoughtfully at him.

He was writing in a small notebook but became conscious of her gaze and looked up.

Surprising her, he said, 'I had a case like this some years ago. Similar history. Young, active woman, sky-high blood pressure. I had a batch of tests done—all negative. She was admitted to hospital six weeks before her due date.'

'And...?'

'She was on complete bed rest and as much medication as was thought safe. She wasn't even allowed out of bed to go to the loo. Everyone was waiting for her to have a massive stroke. She and the baby were monitored constantly. There was talk of a Caesarean, but she vetoed that unless the baby was at risk, but he continued to thrive as the weeks passed.'

Fee's mouth was dry. She licked her lips.

'So what happened?'

'The young mum was bored out of her skull but stuck it out, doing exactly what she was told. She had her first contractions bang on time. It was all textbook stuff. She sailed through each stage and delivered a day earlier than anticipated.'

'And the baby?'

'Perfect—noisy from the word go.'

'And Mum's blood pressure?'

'Returned to normal after a few days. No ill effects—nothing. She's had a couple of other babies since without any marked rise in her blood pressure.'

Fee moved back from the window and sat down again opposite Tom. She switched on a side light and the room was suffused in an orange glow.

Tom looked steadily at her, a faint smile playing round his generously shaped mouth. He could smile, she thought bitterly. He must think it's a big joke. Talk about just retribution. If she had notified him, as she now accepted she should have done—if only out of politeness—with his experience he could have saved her and Jimmy McCallister a load of anxiety.

Because, in spite of what she had told Jimmy and Margot's optimistic attitude, she had been worried. She still would be if this blond giant of a man opposite her hadn't reassured her.

His optimism was securely based on an identical case.

Well, not exactly identical because his patient had been on bed rest, whereas Stella…

'Was it the bed rest that helped, do you think?' Fee asked.

'It's possible, I suppose,' replied Tom, 'but I don't think so. After all, her BP didn't come down until a couple of days after the babe had been born. Your lady's been living a perfectly normal life until recently, but seems none the worse for it. I agree with you that it's a pity she didn't keep up her swimming, since her body was used to that exercise, but apart from that—'

Fee's mobile rang and she fished it out of her pocket.

It was Margot. 'Stella's waters broke a while ago and her contractions have speeded up, but she's beginning to tire a bit,' she said. 'Her BP's staying pretty level and the foetal heartbeat's still strong. I'm just running in some glucose intravenously so that should give her that wee bit extra she needs to keep going.'

'Right. Be there soon.' Fee ended the call and repeated Margot's message to Tom.

His blue eyes seemed to darken and he ran a large hand through his longish blond hair in what Fee interpreted as a nervous gesture. Was he, after all, anxious about Stella and her high blood pressure?

Apparently not, for his next words were again reassuring. 'I don't think that you should worry about her getting tired, Fee,' he said. A wave of pleasure unexpectedly suffused her because he'd called her by her first name. 'After all, most women begin to get exhausted after hours of what must seem unproductive contractions. She'll buck up now that she feels she's getting somewhere—but, then, you know all that.'

He reached out across the table and rested his hand on Fee's. 'Your partner's doing everything that can be done. Look, I don't know if I should offer, or if you'll be offended, but I'm going to risk it and ask if you would like me to go with you. Although I don't think that you need me in the medical sense.' He smiled engagingly. 'But perhaps, on this occasion, a little moral support wouldn't come amiss…?'

So that was what had been making him nervous—the thought of asking her if he might go along for the delivery. She closed her eyes for an instant and made an effort to smother her fears of being taken over. Patients come first, she reminded herself, and if—*if*—anything went wrong, he would be the best person to have around.

She opened her eyes and said, 'Yes, please.'

'Good.'

They were all on their way in five minutes.

Having made up her mind that he should attend the birth, Fee was immensely relieved at the thought of having him there. It had been years since she'd been seriously worried about a delivery, although as Margot often remarked, every birth was different. Perhaps it was because the McCallisters had only just arrived back on Drummock and she hadn't followed the pregnancy through from the word go that she was nervous.

Even the transverse presentation of the Forrester baby hadn't rattled her quite so much, but, then, she'd followed baby Bruce's development since he'd been little more than a pinhead. She had seen him only yesterday and he was like an advertisement for the year's most beautiful baby.

The thought cheered her, and for a moment she forgot that Tom and the children were with her in the car, and sighed happily.

His voice broke in on her thoughts. 'Don't forget to

drop the kids off at Quay House,' he said, his voice full of amusement.

She blushed. 'Sorry! I'm used to driving around on my own, I forgot that I had passengers. The children are so quiet.'

'They're tired,' he said, and groaned theatrically. 'As for me, my ego's cut to the quick that you could forget me. I am surprised.'

Fee was surprised, too, that she had forgotten that he was there. It seemed impossible that she could have overlooked his large physical bulk and his strong...well, *presence*.

She dropped the children off with promises that they could visit her and the chute again, and drove over to the McCallisters' place.

As they drew up in front of the house, Tom said, 'Do you want to go in first and let them know that I'm with you, so that nobody gets any wrong ideas as to why I'm here?' Again that special smile lit up his face and made his eyes glow. 'You know, second doctor called in...'

'The thought had crossed my mind,' agreed Fee. 'Although they are so recently returned from the big city that they might not consider it strange. But we won't take any chances.'

They toasted Lucy Marie McCallister's arrival a couple of hours later. Tom's eyes were suspiciously bright as they met Fee's over the rim of his glass and he mouthed, 'Thank you.'

'Thank you,' she mouthed back at him, and her eyes told him just how much she had appreciated his presence.

CHAPTER TEN

SEVERAL times over the next couple of weeks, Fee was to recall that almost silent vote of thanks from Tom Cameron with something like nostalgia.

For as the days passed and nothing seemed to go right between them, she clung to the memory of those happy moments after the McCallister baby had been born. It had been such a joyful occasion, with her fears of something going wrong with Stella or Lucy Marie laid to rest in Tom's reassuring presence.

Yet he hadn't taken any part in the delivery, he'd just been there. Not that there had been any need for his assistance. As the older midwife had forecast, everything had gone smoothly. The infusion of glucose had helped Stella fight her exhaustion and be alert for the last important contractions.

In theory, this successful episode should have shaped their relationship and made it workable, but from the following day things began to go wrong. Tom's secretary, Kathleen Doughty, who had been a fixture in the practice for years, had dutifully contacted all the patients at present under treatment or booked in for forthcoming surgeries. And yet on that first Monday morning several people turned up at the surgery and were surprised to see Tom in Fee's place.

Most of them accepted that they wouldn't be seeing Nurse McFie, but one woman refused to let Dr Cameron examine her.

'It isna decent,' said Mrs McDonald, a beautifully

groomed old lady in her late eighties who glared at Tom
with dark, beady eyes, 'for a young man to examine an
elderly respectable body old enough to be his granny. I
will see Nurse McFie or nobody!'

Tom bit back an exasperated expletive and said quietly, 'But I'm a qualified doctor, Mrs McDonald, and if
you were in hospital you would be examined by much
younger men than I.'

'Hospitals,' snorted the old lady. 'I don't hold with
those on the mainland, and if I have to go anywhere it'll
be here on Drum, where the young McFie lass and the
other lasses will look after me. Anyway, it's my usual
trouble and she'll know what to do without bothering
about hospitals.'

Well, that was a clue anyway. He brought Mrs
McDonald's case history up on the monitor. Thrush—
both oral and vulvar—had been treated at intervals over
the last year or so, with an antifungoid cream and tablets.
The treatment had been reasonably successful at holding
it at bay, but not in killing the bugs off altogether. About
three months ago a blood test for diabetes had been
taken and had come back negative.

'Where to go from here?' was the rather plaintive
comment typed in beneath the result.

Presumably most of the entries had been made by Fee,
thought Tom, trying to suppress his irritation. Practically
every patient had mentioned her this morning, and with
all the good will in the world he hadn't been able to
prevent her all-pervading presence getting under his
skin.

He tried to be fair. It isn't her fault, he told himself,
that we were both plunged into this situation. If I'd been
properly installed…

Tom steepled his hands beneath his chin and looked

steadily at the elegant elderly patient. Seldom at a loss, he was at one now. He felt frustrated and irritable, not his usual sanguine self at all. Normally he would have dealt with this minor problem with this difficult old lady in no time at all, but this morning…

Of course, there was a reason, although he tried to ignore it. It seemed so feeble. He was missing the children! For the first time in months they would be away from him—away from his protection—for much of the day. It was ridiculous to be afraid for them, but it was exactly six months since tragedy had struck and they'd been at risk. But Drummock, he reminded himself, wasn't an inner-city area. Here they were safe.

Mrs McDonald shifted in her seat and brought him back to earth.

'I can give you the same cream and tablets that Nurse McFie gave you,' he said, despising himself for readily giving in to the patient without a fight. He sat up straight and pulled himself together. 'But you should have more tests done and we should look at your diet. There might be a connection there.'

'Just give me a prescription, please, Doctor,' said Mrs McDonald frostily, standing up and holding out her hand. 'I'll get in touch with Miss McFie.'

'I'll phone her,' said Tom, handing over the prescription, 'and have a word and see if there's anything more we can do to help you.'

He phoned Fee as soon as surgery was over and, not beating about the bush, said briskly, 'Nurse McFie, I had a patient in this morning, a Mrs Monica McDonald—'

'Oh, Lord, I should have warned you about her. Did she refuse to let you examine her?' Her voice was bright and teasing.

'Yes!' He was terse, unable to treat this lightly. 'I

don't like dishing out medication to patients without an examination or knowing their history. But I was virtually forced to or she'd have been stirring up the whole surgery.'

Fee couldn't hold back a chuckle. The thought of the large doctor being forced to succumb to a little old lady, beautifully made up in the manner of a 1940s screen goddess, really was a joke.

'It's not funny,' Tom said sharply. 'If you recall, you didn't think it funny when it happened in reverse and Alice McNabb refused to see you as you weren't a *proper* doctor.'

He regretted the words as soon as he'd uttered them. That had been cruel and unkind and not relevant.

If Fee hadn't carried the load that she had for months, the people of Drummock would have been deprived of constant medical care altogether. And there had been absolutely nothing that he could fault in the treatment she had been giving out. She had picked up a couple of serious conditions which might well have gone undetected for months but for her vigilance.

For some moments the silence from the other end of the phone was deafening, and then Fee said, her voice quiet and controlled, 'You may be assured, Doctor, that from now on I won't play at being a medic, since there's no longer any need. Now, about Mrs Monica McDonald—how can I help you?'

Tom found himself sweating. What damage had he done to their still fragile working relationship? And what effect would it have on their patients—on all the islanders, in fact? It was such a close-knit community. And his sarcastic, totally uncalled-for remark, should it get out, would shatter everything.

He took a shuddering breath. 'I'll never forgive myself for saying that, Fee,' he said in a despairing voice. 'It's a million miles from the truth. You are a doctor *par excellence* even if you haven't got a piece of paper saying so. Everything that I've seen in the notes this morning underlines that. I can't forgive myself but I'm asking you to forgive me.'

'There's nothing to forgive,' came the cool reply. 'I'm not a doctor and have no wish to be. I'm a nurse and proud of it. I have qualifications which enabled me to do a little more when it was necessary, and I'm proud of those, too. Now, to repeat myself, how can I help with Monica McDonald, Dr Cameron?'

Suddenly he felt too tired, too disillusioned to argue or offer any excuses. He felt sick. Drummock, which had seemed so perfect and had offered so much, seemed now anything but. Maybe it was because of the closeness that seemed to have built up during the night. The sun, yesterday golden in a brilliant blue heaven, was now muted and the sky held a greyish tinge.

Many of the people he had seen, especially the older ones, had said that the weather was turning, so maybe that was getting to him. That and the fact that he had spent the morning listening to patients singing Fee's praises and he'd had enough.

'You can help by helping me out here,' he said wearily, 'and giving me a lead as to what I might say or do to put things right. I seem to have done nothing but make a hash of things since I arrived. Is it possible to make a fresh start do you think?'

'I don't know.'

Fee was weary as well, and it sounded in her voice. Had it only been the weekend just past that things had seemed so much better? Showing him the ropes at the surgery and being with the McCallisters for Lucy's arrival, having tea with his children… It had been almost a family weekend.

She had woken that morning feeling light-hearted and optimistic. Perhaps she and Tom could make a go of it after all without treading on each other's toes all the time. But she might have know that it couldn't last. He had gone way beyond mending fences this time. 'I think that the best thing at the moment is for us to each get on with our jobs, and for the patients' sakes to co-operate when necessary,' she said eventually.

'That sounds very cold and businesslike.'

'I'm sorry, it's the best that I can do.'

'The children,' he said hesitantly, 'were thrilled by their visit yesterday and are looking forward to seeing you again.'

It was probably more on account of the chute than her, but a warm flush of pleasure washed over her. 'I enjoyed their company, too. They're lovely kids and they're welcome to come any time.'

'Thank you.'

There was a pause that threatened to go on for a long time, which Fee at last broke. 'Let's get back to Monica McDonald,' she said. 'I presume you're concerned about the recurring bouts of thrush.'

'Yes, and your comment about where to go next.'

'Where would you go?' Fee asked.

'I'd look into her personal hygiene and diet.'

'Her personal hygiene matches what you see on the surface. It's perfect. She's washed and powdered daily to within an inch of her life. Rumour has it that she was the first person on Drummock to have a shower installed. Her house is spotless. She eats well. She's probably a bit short on fruit and veg, but that's nothing out of the way for Drum folk.'

Tom envied her her knowledge of the day-to-day habits of the patients. 'No wonder you were at a loss,' he said. 'I haven't got a clue, except to go for a batch of way-out tests which she ought to have in hospital. You've done the most obvious one—for diabetes.'

'You won't get her into St Cath's, her husband died there some years ago. She sat with him for weeks as he deteriorated. It was the only time in her life that she's left the island.'

'Nurse McFie, I feel an absolute coward, but will you, please, take over the management of this patient, for her sake rather than mine?'

He sweated some more whilst Fee considered her reply. At last she said, 'Several women have asked me if there could be a women's clinic, dealing with female problems.' Her voice, at first sharp, softened a little. 'They have simply got used to having me around, but I think it would be a good idea. Perhaps you would like to mull it over?'

'Perhaps...but will you take over Mrs McDonald?'

'Yes.'

'Thank you. Goodbye.' He put the phone down.

There was nothing more to say.

Fee felt near to tears. After all her efforts to bring them together, she and the doctor looked like being even further apart. She really couldn't ignore his sarcastic remark about her not being a doctor. He was no different to some of the medics on the mainland. It revealed how he really felt about her having filled the role of doctor, although he had made noises of approval about her efforts.

Not only had their relationship been irreparably damaged but it would also prevent her getting to know Simeon and Philly better. Oh, he'd asked if they might be able to visit, but she didn't place much faith in that continuing in the face of the coldness between her and their father.

The weather continued to be grey, and often close and humid.

Fee felt like the weather—tired, breathless and colourless.

She was desperately missing her previous hectic schedule. She wasn't sleeping or eating well and, she realised to her surprise, she was missing her scraps with Tom. Apart from a few strictly work-related exchanges, they had avoided each other assiduously since the fateful phone call.

There was one bright spot when Simeon and Philly rang to tell her how they were getting on at school, and ask if they might visit her at the weekend.

'That would be super,' she said, trying to quell her rising excitement. 'Just let me know when.' Then she added, trying to sound casual, 'How's your father? We haven't seen much of each other, we've both been so busy.'

After a tiny pause, Simeon said, 'Oh, he's OK, a bit tired. He's had a lot of night calls.'

Philly piped up, 'Maggie said that people are taking advantage of him and why can't you do some of the night calls?'

Did she indeed? thought Fee after she'd put the phone down. Well, that was something else she'd have to tackle Maggie about. Perhaps now was the time to broach with her remarks she'd supposedly made about the children.

That evening, when she was sure she would catch Maggie at her own home, Fee called round. As Maggie opened the door, Fee said without preamble, 'Maggie, what the devil have you been telling the doctor? Apparently I'm supposed to have said that his children would be a drag on him. When did I ever say any such thing?'

Maggie appeared unabashed. 'Not in so many words maybe, lass. Don't you remember? It was a couple of days after the doctor arrived. You stopped by for coffee, and said how hard it must be for a man in his position to cope alone with two bairns to bring up.'

Fee clutched her head, now dimly recalling the conversation.

'That's all? I didn't actually call them a "drag"?'

'Of course not.'

'Then how did the children get the idea that I did?'

Maggie's eyes shunned hers for a moment. 'I may have added a touch or two of my own to help make the point.'

Fee stared at her in exasperation. 'But why? Why did you tell any of this to the children? And what do you mean by implying that I'm not prepared to do my share of night calls?'

Maggie sighed. 'Oh, Fiona McFie, where are your wits, girl? I thought that a prod or two coming from the children might push the pair of you in the right direction. It was plain as the nose on your face from the start. He needs you. The two of you belong together!'

Fee walked back home in a daze, her thoughts in turmoil.

So Maggie had been playing matchmaker in her own unique way. Of course, she was a canny old thing, but that didn't make her a romantic counsellor. And although Maggie knew her so well, she couldn't know very much about Tom since she'd only known him a short while. But, then, she did have daily contact with the children, so, no doubt, she had learned a good deal about him from them.

Could it be true? Did Tom really need her support, her *love*, as Maggie had suggested? Her pulses raced at the thought and her spine tingled with pleasure.

Fee suddenly gave a hollow laugh.

What was she thinking of? Even granting that some animal attraction existed between them, they were barely managing to pursue their professional lives without crossing swords. How could they possibly progress to something more meaningful?

A few days later Fee and Tom met unexpectedly at a patient's house. To their surprise they found themselves on the front doorstep together, only to discover that Mrs Stewart, an elderly widow, had called both of them in. She was slightly confused and explained apologetically that she wasn't sure which of them was in charge.

Fee glanced at Tom with a wicked gleam in her eye and hastened to assure Mrs Stewart that Dr Cameron was in charge of prescribing medicine and treatment, and that she as the nurse would carry out his instructions. 'So he's the boss,' she added humbly, tongue in cheek. 'I just do as he tells me.'

Tom glared at her and breathed in heavily. 'We work together as a team,' he said.

Mrs Stewart nodded. 'So it doesn't matter who I call in, then?' she said.

'No,' they agreed in chorus.

Tom followed Fee out when she left and said drily, 'That round to you, I think, Miss McFie.'

But it was as he was getting into his car that Fee chanced to catch the look he gave her. His thoughtful expression had given way to one of admiration...and something else, which unexpectedly made her catch her breath. Then it was wiped away as he realised she had seen him, and he drove off with a curt wave.

Apart from a few similar minor spats whenever they met, an uneasy peace seemed to settle between them. It wasn't very satisfactory, but it was an understanding of sorts and would have to do for the present.

Not long after that Fee held her first women's clinic at the surgery, and was amazed at the number who turned up for it. It was odd that women who could have seen her at any time in the past suddenly discovered a need for advice on intimate female problems. But whatever the reason, Fee was glad to be busy.

She popped over to the hospital to visit the patients and have a word with Jane. Afraid of stepping on Tom's toes, she'd avoided the hospital when possible and hadn't seen Jane for some days, although she had spoken to her on the phone.

The staff nurse greeted her bluntly. 'This isn't going to work, Fee, with you and Tom at loggerheads. He looks awful—you look awful. Why don't you share the practice? Set up some sort of real partnership. It's too big for one person anyway. Dr. Franks only survived as long as he did because you shouldered much of the work, even before he got so frail. And the population has grown since then.'

'There's not a chance of us sharing,' said Fee. 'We don't agree on anything—well, rarely. Tom doesn't approve of nurses playing at doctors.'

'Did he say that?'

'Not in so many words, but he implied it.'

'Then snap out of whatever's bugging you and get your act together!' Jane said, surprisingly sharply.

'I'd better go,' said Fee abruptly. At the door she paused. 'What do you mean, "at loggerheads"? Is it as obvious as that? We've been keeping apart as much as possible.'

'I rest my case,' said Jane.

The storm broke with startling suddenness two days later.

Fee was on the coast road on the Atlantic side of the island when she noticed the line of purple-black clouds rising ominously over the western horizon. Obviously a storm was coming in.

'There goes my holiday,' she muttered.

She had intended to go swimming. After the unseasonably mild weather, courtesy of the Gulf Stream, which had carried right on into November, the sea had remained warm enough for bathing—as long as one didn't stay in too long.

Taking a 'holiday' in November would normally not have been on her agenda, but Jane's blunt accusation had found its mark and she had arranged a day off to think through the situation between herself and Tom. It had to be resolved. If Jane had noticed their estrangement then other people probably had, too. There was a definite hint in the air of two camps emerging, and it wouldn't do.

She drove slowly on as her time was her own, watching the thickening clouds flickering with flashes of distant lightning. The only good thing, she mused, was her growing friendship with Simeon and Philly. They came over at the weekends and sometimes after school when their father was taking a late surgery, or when Maggie had a friend visiting and was having what Simeon described, in affectionate imitation of Maggie, as 'a wee bit o' good gossip'.

They brought their homework with them and made no fuss about doing it. But when they had finished, they couldn't wait to rummage through the old toy box that Fee had clung onto for sentimental reasons. It was full of old board games, some of which had belonged to her parents and which filled them with delight. They whiled away the dark evenings playing ludo and snakes and ladders, and other family board games.

They were happy evenings, thought Fee, marred only by Tom's absence and the void between them. On one occasion, when she had walked the children home, they had met at his front door and they had exchanged stilted greetings. She wondered if the children had noticed, or if Tom had said anything to them to indicate his feelings. But she wouldn't probe—that would smack of invading his privacy.

Fee came out of her reverie as she realised how dark it had suddenly become.

The last slivers of blue sky were shrinking away to the east, obscured by a swirling, billowing grey blanket covering the sky. The storm was coming up unusually fast! An eye-searing sheet of lightning blazed overhead, making Fee flinch, followed only scant seconds later by a deafening boom that rumbled away across the island with ground-shaking force.

A gust of wind hit the side of her car hard enough to make it rock wildly, forcing her to jerk at the steering wheel to stay on the road.

Then the rain started—a few huge drops breaking on the windscreen, merging in seconds into a solid hissing, roaring, wind-driven downpour that drummed on the car roof. The windscreen wipers couldn't cope with the deluge and she pulled to the side and stopped as the road ahead vanished in a blur of grey.

She shivered and pulled on her coat, suddenly aware of how cold it had become. She didn't remember hearing about this on the weather forecast that morning...but that had been a few hours ago. She switched on her car radio and hunted for any weather news. The reception was deteriorating rapidly, interspersed with dramatic pops and crackles, synchronised with the flashes of lightning now playing all about her.

Suddenly she found what she was after.

'The remnants of a hurricane which devastated America's east coast a few days ago...strengthened by unusually warm waters in the North Atlantic... predicted to pass north and west of the Hebrides, has turned East in the last few hours... picked up speed...threatening Northern Ireland and the west coast of Scotland...severe weather warnings have gone out to all coastal regions and sea areas...'

Fee turned the radio off.

This was obviously going to be a serious storm. She'd better get home. They might need extra help at the hospital.

She put on her headlights, started up the car and began crawling forward through the driving rain and spray to the next passing place where she could turn round. She couldn't remember when she'd seen weather so foul.

Just as she reached a passing place, the distorted headlights of a vehicle coming toward her suddenly loomed out of the torrential downpour. She jammed on the brakes, narrowly avoiding skidding into Tom's Range Rover. There was hardly room for them both on the tiny road and they barely scraped past each other, pulling up so that their driver's doors were only inches apart. They wound down the windows and shouted at each other through the hissing curtain of rain.

'I've got a young lad named Colin Webster in the back with an appendix about ready to pop,' Tom said urgently.

'I know him,' Fee shouted back. 'Stays with his grandmother along the Windings.'

'Yes, she called me after he was violently sick. Severe abdominal pain and all the symptoms of appendicitis. I gave him a shot of morphine and loaded him up. He's got to get to St Cath's urgently. I've been trying to get the air ambulance service but no joy. Maybe my phone's on the blink. Will you try them and follow me along? I'm making for the helipad.'

'Will do.' Fee nodded. 'You go ahead and I'll turn round.'

As she drove she called the helicopter service on her mobile, but got only static. She tried the hospital with the same result. In the distance well ahead of her she could just make out the blurred taillights of the Range Rover. She tried Tom's mobile number—more static. The whole mobile net must be down, she thought.

Fee went as fast as she dared to catch up with Tom. There was no point in heading for the helipad if they couldn't contact the service. If his brief description of the state of the lad's appendix was accurate, and she was sure that it was, then time was of the essence.

The road dropped down towards the shore and Fee glimpsed the sea. Huge white-capped waves whipped up by the wind were crashing onto a tiny beach, their raw power and fury suddenly frightening. Again the howling wind buffeted her car and she had to struggle to keep control, slowing to a virtual crawl. She snatched another glance at the great humpbacked swell of the ocean rolling toward the shore, lit up almost continuously by lightning. It wouldn't be long before the coast road was submerged as the sea overran it. She had a picture of the island surrounded by monstrous seas, turning the sound into a seething maelstrom.

She managed to close the distance between herself and Tom and flashed her lights until he pulled over. She drew up beside him, reached over and wound down her passenger window, letting in a spray of rain and wind.

'I can't get through!' she shouted. 'We'll have to go to the hospital first and call from there. The land line should still be working. We can make Colin comfortable while we wait.'

'OK!' he bellowed back.

A little way on they turned off the coast road and Fee followed Tom along the lane leading around the back of the township to the hospital. The wind shrilled around her car, setting it rocking alarmingly, and she had to fight to keep it on the road.

Only then did the full significance of their situation dawn on her. She realised the sickening truth that it didn't matter whether they could raise the mainland or not.

There were only two ways off Drummock—by sea or by air.

Only a large ship could safely navigate in these conditions and even then to come into harbour would be tricky. A few years ago the ferry had had to turn back to the mainland rather than risk docking in weather less severe than this. As for aircraft, regular helicopters wouldn't fly up in these conditions. A big military craft might be powerful enough, but she wasn't sure. That only left fixed-wing craft. She saw rivulets streaming off the hillside and knew that the field set aside as an emergency landing ground would already be awash. It was only long enough for single-engined aircraft to land, and even if they reached the island they might flip over if their wheels sank into saturated ground. Nothing big enough to weather the storm could possibly touch down in safety.

They were physically cut off from the outside world as long as the storm lasted.

Normally that would only be a minor inconvenience. But now they had a boy who had to be operated upon within a couple of hours at the outside. If nothing was done for him, his appendix would burst, septicaemia would set in and he would almost certainly die!

CHAPTER ELEVEN

FEE forced herself to think calmly as she drove on through the howling storm.

If Colin couldn't be transported safely to the mainland, they would have to operate on him here. There was no other alternative—but was it possible?

Normally they only performed the most minor surgery, small biopsies and suchlike. On previous occasions, when it had been considered safer for an op to be done without moving the patient, the day surgery unit had been converted into an operating theatre, and a full complement of trained staff, including an anaesthetist, had come over from the mainland. Although an appendicectomy was a simple operation in principle, it still required the proper staff and equipment.

Was Tom capable of operating? All medics had some degree of surgical experience, but did he have enough? And even then, they would have to operate using a local anaesthetic and a general sedative only. It was the only way if they were to save the boy's life.

The hospital loomed out of the billowing veil of rain and they drew up outside the entrance, Tom sounding his horn to attract the attention of the staff. Fee scrambled out of her car and ran to help Tom with his patient. The awning over the hospital entrance gave them some slight shelter from the driving rain, though Fee heard it creaking and groaning under the ferocious wind. As Tom opened up the back of Range Rover she saw Colin's pale, sweating face. His eyes were closed and he appeared to be only half-conscious.

Tom gently, almost effortlessly lifted his young patient from the back of his car. At that moment Joe Drummond appeared beside him with a wheelchair.

'Thought I might be needed here when this started to blow up,' he said tersely by way of explanation.

Tom placed his patient in the wheelchair, Fee covered him with a blanket and they all hurried inside. The warmth and light of the tiny hospital enveloped them as the doors shut, muting the noise of the raging storm. Jane was waiting for them. Tom briefed her on Colin's condition as she whisked him into the ward.

Meanwhile Fee made for the office telephone.

When Tom and Jane entered the office ten minutes later, Fee was just replacing the receiver. The look on her face said it all.

'We can't expect any help for six hours at least, probably much longer,' she said simply. 'The storm's sudden change in course has caught everybody by surprise, and there are emergencies of one kind or another all round the coast. Lifeboats and air-sea rescue are already working at full stretch. Everything else is making for port or grounded. We're on our own.'

Tom broke the strained silence that followed her announcement.

'We all know Colin won't last six hours. There's no other choice, is there? I'm going to have to operate.'

Half an hour later a larger group had gathered in the office. In addition to Tom, Fee and Jane, there were two nurses, Joe and Andrew Crawford in his capacity as the local pharmacist. He had brought with him a large case of medical supplies.

Outside the wind howled and shrieked, rattling the

windows. Every so often the lights flickered. The town, lying in the hollow of the harbour bay, was relatively sheltered. It was far worse on exposed ground or out at sea.

Tom perched himself on the edge of the desk and motioned to everyone to find seats. He looks as if that's where he belongs, thought Fee.

'Thank you all for coming in at short notice,' he said. 'I'll be as quick as I can since time is of the essence. I presume that you all know the basic fact that we are going to operate under a local anaesthetic to remove a badly infected appendix about to perforate?'

There was a murmur of confirmation.

He put his palms together as if praying, and looked thoughtful. 'Although an appendicectomy is normally a straightforward piece of surgery, to remove an appendix in these conditions, even under a general anaesthetic, would be tricky; doing it under a local isn't going to be a picnic. But we can't afford to wait. If it bursts, Colin will probably die of septicaemia.'

He parted his hands and ran his fingers through his mop of flaxen hair. It needs cutting, thought Fee. 'If we operate, we run all kinds of risks, not least that of nicking the swollen appendix and setting free the contents…but I don't need to go into that.

'In spite of the risks, it's my professional opinion that we have no choice but to operate. You may feel differently, so if any of you are unsure and don't want to be involved, please, back out now, because once we get cracking everyone will have an important role to play and it'll be too late.'

Nobody moved or said anything and he smiled his thanks and spoke to Fee and the nurses.

'I know that you'll get things set up,' he said. 'Obviously the day surgery has to be cleaned to as near operating-theatre standards as we can manage in the time. In addition, I need the largest-size gloves and whatever instruments you can rustle up for a normal excision of an appendix, plus any more that might be useful. And, of course, whatever local anaesthetics and sedatives Mr Crawford and I come up with.'

Half an hour later they were ready. In the background waged one of the most ferocious storms in living memory, though Drummock was no stranger to storms. The noise was so loud that at times it made conversation difficult.

Fee would be assisting Tom, and she took up her position opposite him at the table. Jane acted as theatre nurse, presiding over a trolley laden with instruments.

One of the other nurses, a young woman recently trained in Edinburgh, was ready to pick up and count dirty swabs and generally fetch and carry. The other nurse was to be on hand to act as resuscitation nurse once the operation was over. Andrew remained in theatre, too, ready to assist with the array of local anaesthetics and sedatives that he and Tom considered necessary.

Fee looked round and was proud of the makeshift team.

The young nurse, Angie, who, until she had married a Drummock man and come to live on the island, had planned a career in Theatre, was full of confidence. But Jane, who was much more aware of all the things that could go wrong, confessed to Fee as they scrubbed up before the op, 'I'll probably drop everything in sight.'

'You and me both,' said Fee.

Jane snorted in derision. 'I don't believe that for a moment. You're as cool as the boss man is.'

'It's all front,' said Fee with a chuckle. 'I did a special
stint in Theatre for my last qualification, but that was
with all the usual back-up of hospital facilities and, anyway, it was years ago.'

They moved into the theatre where Joe, helped by
Angie and the other nurse, had placed a heavily sedated
but still conscious Colin on the operating table.

Fee cast a final eye round to make sure that all was
well and gave the thumbs-up sign.

'Right,' she said. 'Now all we want is the man himself.'

Tom had a surprise for them as he made the first incision. His hand was perfectly steady as he cut firmly but
with infinite care into the taut, inflamed flesh over the
appendix. Fee mopped up the trickle of blood with a
forceps-held swab and then gently retracted the first
layer of skin. Now that they had started she felt completely at home and at ease. This man knew what he was
doing and she was competent to help him.

'The last time I did a similar op under a local anaesthetic,' Tom said, his blue eyes glinting above his mask,
'was in a very shaky old cargo boat in the middle of a
storm. I was earning my passage as ship's surgeon.'

'And I bet you weren't as well equipped as we are,'
quipped Fee, wondering if there was a word of truth in
what he was saying or if he was just spinning a tale to
keep everyone relaxed.

'That,' he murmured, 'is very true. This is luxury
compared to what was available on that occasion.'

It was impossible to tell if he was simply kidding.
Was there any truth in this story, or was it just a way of
boosting morale at this critical point in the operation?
Perhaps he was bolstering his own morale. The next few

minutes were certainly going to be crucial. One tremor of those large hands…the incision a fraction too deep…

Tom was already cutting into the next layer of skin and muscle, his beautiful hands manipulating the scalpel with delicate precision. He glanced at Colin's face and chest, noting that his colour was as good as could be expected and his respirations were fairly even. The mix of painkillers and sedatives they had given him were working like a dream.

Moments later Fee retracted the deeper layer of skin and muscle that he'd freed, exposing a well of blood. She used suction to steadily remove the blood as well as swabbing as fast as she could. It seemed a heart-stoppingly slow procedure when time was so valuable, but Tom couldn't see what he was doing until she had got most of it away. A dark blob slowly became visible—a time bomb that was the infected appendix.

Everyone held their breath.

Outwardly Tom looked cool and collected, but across the table Fee could feel the tension flowing round him. Now was the crucial moment. One wrong stroke of the scalpel and the swollen appendix might burst, spilling its poisonous contents into the abdominal cavity.

'Moment of truth,' he muttered so that only Fee could hear. But his large gloved hands didn't waver as he carefully snipped free the pus-filled bag and dropped it gently into the stainless-steel receiver that Jane placed before him.

'Refrigerate that until it can go off for examination,' he said.

He washed out the open incision, inserted a drain tube, applied penicillin liberally and began closing up, stitching the layers of flesh back into place with great care. When the last stitch was in place and the thread cut,

Tom backed away from the table, took off his gloves and mask and with deliberation threw them into the disposal bin.

'OK, you can move him back to the ward now. I'll be in the office, writing up my notes, if you need me.' He smiled at them. 'I think we did it.'

The tension broke and suddenly the room was full of laughing people grinning foolishly under their masks.

Twenty minutes later, Fee came into the office to find Tom finishing his notes. The small room seemed oddly peaceful. Outside the storm continued to rage, but Tom had somehow cocooned himself within a bubble of studious concentration which was almost palpable.

Fee looked uncertainly at the big blond man hunched over the desk. In spite of the fact that she had just witnessed him performing surgery under the most trying conditions and was admiring him for his medical expertise, her personal feelings were ambivalent. Was it because they'd had such a bad start to their working relationship that she didn't quite *trust* him? No, that wasn't the word, but for the life of her she couldn't think what was.

Today in Theatre he had treated her with all the respect that was proper toward a medical colleague, yet still… It was almost as if she was afraid to let him come closer. But that was nonsense. Why should she be afraid of him?

Tom looked up at her. 'How's Colin doing?' he asked.

'Fine. As comfortable as can be expected, anyway. I've told the nurse specialling him that one of us must be called if there's any change in his condition.'

She wondered for a moment if he would comment on

their shared responsibility for Colin, but he merely nodded.

'Good. I think, as long as we don't get any more emergencies like that, we should be able to see this through.'

A sudden thought stuck Fee. 'Your children—'

'I called Maggie before we operated,' Tom said smoothly. 'She said she'd make sure they got home from school safely. Sounded as though she was taking all this in her stride.'

Fee smiled. 'People on Drummock know what to do in a storm like this. You don't fret about what you can't fight. You sit tight, keep your head down and be patient. It'll pass. Things always do.'

Tom smiled. 'That's not a bad philosophy for life as a whole. Except that sometimes you've got to put your head up and take a risk.'

'It's served us well enough for hundreds of years,' Fee said defensively.

Before Tom could reply the office phone rang. Tom answered. He listened in silence to the voice at the other end for thirty or so seconds, and Fee saw his lips pinch together. Then he said simply, 'Right, we'll be ready.' And hung up.

'That was the harbourmaster's office,' he said. 'A ship running from the storm has just hit the harbour wall. We'd better get ready to receive casualties!'

As they found out later, the vessel was a small coastal cargo carrier named *The Bryony Lady*. Caught by the sudden speed of the storm and with damaged steering, the captain had tried to make for the nearest safe harbour, which turned out to be Drummock. They had almost made it, but a huge wave had caught them just as they were passing through the harbour mouth, dashing them against the quay wall. What had made the accident worse had been that when they'd hit, several of the crew had been down in the hold trying to secure some cargo which had come loose and had threatened the stability of the ship.

Joe Drummond went down to the harbour as soon as the news had come through. Meanwhile Tom gathered the rest of the staff.

'I don't know if anyone has been injured,' he told them, 'and I won't waste time going down to see. There are plenty of people around more competent than me to help on the spot. We can rely on Joe and his colleagues to get any casualties up here as soon as possible. The best thing we can do is prepare for the worst.' He looked at Jane. 'Will you be able to cope if several cases need to be hospitalised?' he asked her.

'We've two beds immediately available in the ward. No problem to put up another three in there if necessary. If we need more, we might have to use the waiting area, as we did last year during the flu epidemic. That wouldn't be too difficult, provided that we have the staff.'

'I'll start calling up volunteers while the ordinary phones are still working,' Fee said.

'Don't you worry, Doctor,' Jane told Tom. 'We've managed before and we'll do it again.'

'That's the Drummock spirit,' said Tom.

The next few hours passed in dealing with a succession of injuries as crewmen were pulled from the hold of the foundering ship. Off-duty staff poured in from all over the island and quickly made themselves useful, leaving Fee free to directly assist Tom in attending to the more severely injured. But there was a limit to what they could do. In some cases all they could do was make the patients as comfortable as possible until the storm passed and they could be transferred to St Cath's.

One of the senior staff nurses acted as triage nurse and sorted the minor injuries from those more severe. Mostly they were lacerations, crushing injuries and broken bones. The simple breaks were dealt with by a helper who turned out to have been a plaster nurse in a London hospital before she'd retired to Drummock.

The local talent was amazing, thought Tom. Andrew made himself generally useful. As well as being the town pharmacist, he was a senior officer in the St Andrew's Ambulance Association and certainly knew his stuff. Again he assisted Tom and Fee in their makeshift theatre work, planning the most suitable mixture of sedation and painkillers for each patient. When he wasn't needed there he helped in the ward.

They soon filled the available beds and within an hour nurses were busy setting up more. Not long after that, the waiting room was taken over.

At some point during that crazy period, when they worked like a conveyor-belt system in a factory, they snatched a few minutes for a teabreak in the office next to the theatre. Tom phoned home to find out how the children were getting along. After he'd spoken to Maggie, who told him that the children had been safely collected from school by her brother, Tom had a word with Simeon and Philly.

They were full of the excitement of coming home with Sam. 'He carried us part of the way,' said Simeon, 'because the puddles were too deep and the water would have come over the top of our wellies, especially over Philly's because she's little. She almost got blown over by the wind. The garden's like a lake,' he continued breathlessly. 'I wanted to make a raft and punt about on it but Maggie says that it's not deep enough for that and it will be dark soon.'

Nearly dark? Tom felt disorientated. 'What time is it?' he asked automatically, feeling foolish at having to ask such a thing of his young son. It was odd, but all the time he'd been treating people he'd kept checking the clock to see how long each process was taking, but the actual time hadn't registered.

'Just after four o'clock,' replied Simeon. 'Philly wants to speak to you, Dad,' he added.

It was incredible, hearing their excited voices. To them it was all a great big adventure whereas for himself and Fee it was sheer hard work, spiced with the fear that something might go wrong whilst they were tending a patient with less than adequate equipment.

Philly's happy voice came over the crackly receiver. 'Is Fee with you?' she wanted to know.

'Yes,' replied Tom. 'We've been working together all day.' He glanced across at Fee, who was sipping tea from a mug held in both hands. Her theatre cap was pushed back on her ruffled red-gold hair and her eyes were closed. Her face was pale and there was a sheen of sweat on it.

Tight fingers seemed to close round Tom's heart and he had to fight for breath. They had worked together side by side for hours, occasionally touching, occasionally smiling at each other. Occasionally he had felt her tremble and her lovely eyes had held an expression of such tenderness in them that a lump had come into his throat.

This wasn't the tough professional woman who had been fighting him every inch of the way since he'd come to Drummock. This was the tender, soft, womanly woman who had been there all the time, hidden beneath a veneer of toughness. The part of her, he now realised, that she'd had to suppress to do the job that duty had demanded of her.

And at that moment he knew that this was the woman he'd fallen utterly, completely and irrevocably in love with. The woman he was going to marry, the woman who was going to be mother to his children. Yes, they would have children of their own, his and Fee's...

'Daddy, are you there?' said Philly's voice urgently.

'Yes, poppet, I'm here.'

'Will you give Fee my love and tell her that I've nearly finished the—? Oh it's a secret from you. It's to do with Christmas, but she'll know.'

Tom's heart thumped unevenly at the thought of his daughter sharing a secret with Fee, especially a secret that concerned him. Like a real mother and daughter, he thought, and immediately berated himself for being so sentimental.

He cleared his throat. 'I'll pass on the message,' he said. 'Take care, both of you, and do what you can to help Maggie.' He replaced the receiver and looked across the room, to find Fee's beautiful eyes on him.

'All well?' she asked softly.

Some primitive instinct told him that she meant more than the children's immediate welfare. She had read him like a book, was privy to all his most private thoughts.

'All well,' he replied.

CHAPTER TWELVE

It was late that evening before Fee and Tom finished treating the last of the injured crewmen. They had worked together all day as if they had worked together for years, each anticipating the other's needs. Only when the long day ended and a wild, storm-tossed night had closed over the island could they find a few minutes alone in the office.

Fee was weary but elated. She turned to look at Tom. His eyes were on her. He was smiling his wide, generous smile that made the corners of his vivid blue eyes crinkle at the corners. The bright overhead strip light threw his nose and stubble-covered chin into relief. He needed a shave.

'That's how you smiled at me the day we met,' she said softly.

'Moonstones!' he exclaimed in an awed voice, taking a step toward her. 'Your eyes are like moonstones, an almost translucent green-blue.'

The moonstone eyes widened. Tom moved closer to her. He cupped her face in his large hands, and his thumbs caressed her cheekbones. It felt incredibly intimate and sexy.

He said in a low voice, 'I love you, Fiona McFie, and my children love you—and if I had a dog and a cat they would love you, too. Will you marry me?'

Had he really said that? he wondered. It was the sort of nonsense stuff that came into one's head during the night watches.

Her beautiful eyes told him that he *had* spoken out loud. They were huge in the pale oval of her face. She looked stunned, as well she might. One might think in that kind of fanciful language, but one didn't say it out aloud—except in unusual circumstances.

Tom consoled himself with the thought that these were unusual circumstances.

He dropped a kiss on her forehead and murmured, 'Have I blown it, Fee? Have I jumped the gun? Are you asking yourself how you could marry a man who's daft enough to propose amongst bloodstained dressings, after one hell of a day's work?'

Fee gently tugged his hands from her face and shook her head.

'No, I'm wondering if you really mean it or if you're a little light-headed. It can easily happen in the dead of night.'

She was giving him an 'out' he realised, a chance to take back his words about moonstones and marriage.

'You mean that we say and do foolish things or, in a curious way, one dares to say things that one wouldn't normally.'

'Either—both,' she said, a smile hovering at the corners of her mouth.

Tom placed his hands on her shoulders. 'I mean every word of it, Fee, and when this lot is over…' he waved a hand toward the rattling windows '…I will repeat my proposal in the broad, sober light of day.'

Fee believed him and couldn't wait for the broad light of day.

It didn't matter that out of the blue their relationship had suddenly catapulted into a new dimension which only days ago had seemed an impossible dream. Now she realised it had been there from the start, simmering beneath the tension that had existed between them from the moment he'd arrived on the island.

'Perhaps we should have known all along,' she said with a tired laugh. 'Two people who argued as much as we did had to have *something* in common…'

It was early next morning when the wind and rain stopped almost as abruptly as they had begun, leaving behind an eerie, unearthly silence.

The absence of noise woke Tom, who'd been snatching a couple of hours' sleep in the duty room. For a moment he lay quite still, hardly daring to breathe. The cessation of the storm's wailing was extraordinary. He slid off the camp bed and made his way to the ward office.

Fee was there, her pen poised over a patient's notes, the soft contours of her face lit by the desk lamp. 'Has it really stopped?' she whispered.

Tom nodded. 'Yes, isn't it wonderful?'

'Wonderful.' He perched himself on the edge of the desk and leaned over to kiss her on the top of her head. 'We can start living again and I can finish some unfinished business.'

With the dawn and the dying down of the storm came the first of the helicopters to carry the sick and injured away to St Cath's. News was also received that a salvage tug had been despatched to help clear the half-submerged hulk of *The Bryony Lady* from the harbour.

Meanwhile the people of the island began clearing up the damage the storm had left behind. There was surprisingly little of it, considering the battering the island had taken. The mostly low, solid buildings had suffered far less than modern structures would have done.

It was early afternoon, when routine had been reestablished once more and all patients were comfortable, before Tom left the hospital and made his way back to Quay House.

Simeon and Philly met him at the door, relieved to see him and excited at the same time.

'We watched them rescuing the people from the ship that hit the harbour wall,' Simeon babbled, as they led Tom inside to the warmth of the kitchen. 'We could see almost everything from upstairs. They had lights going all through the night, even though it was raining so hard.'

'The wind kept rattling the windows, but I wasn't scared,' Philly interjected proudly.

'That was very brave of you,' Tom said, kissing her on the forehead.

'Maggie said you and Fee were working very hard at the hospital.' Simeon said. He hesitated. 'Nobody…died, did they?'

'No,' Tom said, 'nobody died.' He took a deep breath. 'But something important did happen. Let's all sit down for a minute. I want to talk to you about Fee…'

An hour later, Fee answered a knock at her door to find Tom, Philly and Simeon standing there.

'Let's go for a walk,' Tom said simply.

They walked along the beach. The sun was surprisingly warm, shining out of a cloudless aquamarine sky washed clear by the recent rain.

Tom took Fee's hand. She thrilled at his touch, tingling with awareness. A shiver rippled up her spine. I love him so much that it hurts, she thought.

'Almost worth a hurricane to have all this,' he said, swinging her hand high as they strode along the sandy shoreline. The children ran ahead of them, examining

the shells and other flotsam the storm had left behind.
Watching their innocent play, Tom said suddenly,
'Drummock is an island made for romance!'

He gave a bellow of laughter, took Fee by the waist
and swung her round as if she were a child.

He looked and sounded boyish, a far cry from the
dedicated doctor of the last few days. The tired lines had
almost disappeared from his open handsome face and
the wide forehead. His blue shirtsleeves were rolled up,
exposing strongly muscled forearms. His blond hair
looked white in the sunshine.

They reached the spot where two months ago they had
watched from their cars as the children had played in
the sea. Tom sat down and propped himself against an
ancient rowan tree that grew on a spit of land jutting out
into the Atlantic.

He patted the sand beside him and brushed aside some
battered reddish-orange berries that had been torn off the
tree by the wind.

'Come,' he said softly.

Fee sank down beside him and he cradled her head
against his broad chest. She could hear his rhythmic
heartbeat.

His arm tightened round her and he mumbled into her
freshly shampooed, scented hair, 'You know that I'm
head over heels in love with you, Fee, don't you?'

She smiled and planted a kiss on the underside of his
stubbly chin, which was the easiest point to reach. She
laughed softly. 'Your midnight proposal more or less
clinched it. But I think I knew before then, but I simply
couldn't admit it to myself.'

He laughed delightedly. 'You're psychic, Miss McFie,
and have a delicious sense of humour. But you can't
know how much I love you. Not sensibly or practically

as a man crashing forty should, but madly—like a man half my age.'

His dazzling blue eyes sparkled like sapphires. 'So will you marry me, my dearest…?' he brushed his lips across her forehead '…darling…' he kissed her nose '…lovely lady?'

'You know, I think I will.' She gave a husky little laugh. 'I shall have the best of both worlds, a mature man and a young lover.'

She sat up and moved slightly away from him.

'Hey, come back,' he murmured, reaching out for her.

Fee shook her head. 'We should talk,' she said.

'You want to know more about me before you commit yourself?'

She shook her head again. 'I'm already committed,' she said, 'but I want to know more about you, because lovers always want to know more about their loved one.' She sifted silver sand between her fingers. 'If they don't, they can't be in love.'

Tom raised her sandy hand to his lips and kissed it. 'I'll go along with that. One of the most delightful things about falling in love with you, my dearest Fee, has been hearing tales of what you were like when you were a little girl.'

'And there you have the advantage of me, Tom. I know nothing about you except that you are a widower and had a GP practice in London.'

Tom raised his eyebrows in surprise. 'But surely the kids have filled you in?'

'I could sense they were reticent about their past and I didn't push them. I felt that it smacked of probing, taking advantage of their innocence. I suppose I knew that in time you would tell me all that you wanted me to know.'

Tom kissed her palm and then each fingertip in turn.

'Fiona McFie, has anyone ever told you that, as well as being stunningly beautiful, you are a remarkably sensible and honourable woman?' His voice was deep and husky.

Her lovely eyes, mirroring the blue green ocean, danced. 'Well, not in those words exactly,' she replied with a dimpling grin. She tugged her hand gently away from his. 'But it doesn't mean that I'm not bursting with curiosity…no, not curiosity but a longing to know everything about you.'

'Everything! Tall order.'

She hugged her knees and stared out to sea. 'I don't want every detail right at this moment. If there's anything you don't want to tell, then don't. But there are a couple of things to which I would really like answers…even if it is a little painful.'

'Go on.'

'How and when did your wife die? And was her death the reason you moved to Scotland?'

Tom looked away into the distance, then said quietly, 'She died in a car accident. That was nearly three years ago.' His voice tightened. 'In fact, she wasn't much of a mother or wife. Just as well in a way as the children didn't seem to miss her that much when she was gone. She was beautiful, but the beauty was only skin deep. Unfortunately, by the time I found that out Simeon was on the way, so I stuck to it and hoped for the best. But she was restless, often taking herself off at short notice to stay with friends—and one friend in particular. He was the one driving the car when she died.'

His voice faded for a moment as he tried to get himself under control.

'So you decided to move to forget.'

'Partly that and also to get away from my solo practice. I needed time for the children. I told you about the break-in. The kids were terrified and it made the house seem, well, dirty. Afterwards it didn't seem like our home. That decided me.'

An expression of anguish flitted across his face and his lips set into a thin line. He shivered as if he were suddenly cold.

'That's why, on that first morning, you said that all you wanted was that your children should be safe. Do you remember?

Tom nodded.

Fee leaned over and gave him a long, lingering kiss, gentle but firm, brushing her warm, soft lips against his tight, cool mouth. 'Tom, don't go on if it hurts too much, my darling. There's no need.'

A tide of intense tenderness washed through her and her heart tumbled around in her chest. She rolled out of her sitting position, knelt in front of him and cupped his strong chin in her hands. He caught her wrists and held them.

'Do you really love me that much?' he murmured, his eyes searching her face.

'I really love you that much,' she replied, dropping more kisses on his forehead, nose and cheeks whilst smoothing the shadows beneath his eyes with her thumbs.

He eased her hands from his face and folded them between his own.

'Then something happened that finally took the decision to move out of my hands. I picked up a tropical bug from one of my Asian patients. I was on the critical list for a time and I was sent to Switzerland to a hospital where they specialised in exotic diseases. The director

and his wife turned out to be people I'd been to med
school with. Really nice people. They offered to have
the children while I was hospitalised.'

He shrugged his wide shoulders. 'It turned out to be
the best thing the kids could have had, taking them right
away from the last few traumatic years. I promised them
that when I was well enough we would move out of
London and go somewhere as beautiful as Switzerland.'

Fee unbuttoned his shirt and kissed the exposed tri-
angle of warm brown flesh down to the waistband of his
trousers. 'So that's where you got your gorgeous tan.'

'Hussy.' Tom chuckled, trying to pull his shirt together and answer her question. 'Yes, the hospital had
once been a TB sanatorium. It was all balconies and
wide windows looking out across the mountains. The
view alone was a tonic. When I began to recover, I
vowed to find somewhere like that for us to live. Then
I saw the advertisement for the Drummock post. It was
out of date by then, but I took a chance…and the rest,
as they say, you know.'

Fee stopped teasing and whispered, 'Another miracle.
Your guardian angel must have been watching over
you…and St Drum, of course. He must have known that
we needed you here.'

Tom said softly. 'I think both our guardian angels
have been working overtime lately.' He crushed her
against his chest and gave her a long, hard kiss.

Fee came up gasping for air. 'Wow, that was quite a
kiss, Dr Cameron.'

'I've an endless supply of those,' he said. 'Enough to
last a lifetime. But do you think Drummock will accept
me if I marry her favourite daughter?'

Fee smiled. 'After the work you've done in the last
twenty-four hours, I don't think anybody will dare say

a word against you. They'll have me to reckon with if they do!'

Tom rolled over and stood up abruptly, then held out his hand and pulled her to her feet. 'Come on,' he said. 'Let's go and give the kids the good news.'

Fee tugged her hand free. 'Oh no,' she exclaimed. 'You must break it to them gently. Discuss it with them first. We might have to work on the idea of us getting married for a long time. No way must they feel pressured into accepting me as your wife.'

Tom grasped her arm. 'No question of that.' He was laughing. 'I've already told them I was going to ask you. They seem to think that you would make quite a good mum.'

A short distance away Simeon and Philly were paddling in the shallow water. Tom called out to them and the children turned and came running toward them.

'Have you asked Fee?' they shouted as they got nearer. 'And did she say—?'

'*Yes*,' sang out Fee, running to meet them. 'I said yes!'

Two sturdy bodies thudded into her and she put her arms round them and hugged them.

Tom strode up and put his arms round all three of them. 'We're home at last,' he said softly.

Modern Romance™
...seduction and
passion guaranteed

Tender Romance™
...love affairs that
last a lifetime

Medical Romance™
...medical drama on
the pulse

Historical Romance™
...rich, vivid and
passionate

Sensual Romance™
...sassy, sexy and seductive

27 new titles every month.

*With all kinds of Romance for
every kind of mood...*

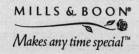

MILLS & BOON®

Makes any time special™

MAT4RS

GIVE US YOUR THOUGHTS

Mills & Boon® want to give you the best possible read, so we have put together this short questionnaire to understand exactly what you enjoy reading.

Please tick the box that corresponds to how appealing you find each of the following storylines.

32 Richmond Square

They're fab, fashionable – and for rent. When the apartments in this central London location are let, the occupants find amazing things happen to their love lives. The mysterious landlord always makes sure that there's a happy ending for everyone who comes to live at number 32.

How much do you like this storyline?

❑ Strongly like   ❑ Like   ❑ Neutral – neither like nor dislike

❑ Dislike   ❑ Strongly dislike

Please give reasons for your preference:

_____

_____

The Marriage Broker

This city agency matches marriage partners for practical as well as emotional reasons. Upmarket, discreet and with an international clientele, The Marriage Broker offers a personal service to match clients' needs and situations.

How much do you like this storyline?

❑ Strongly like   ❑ Like   ❑ Neutral – neither like nor dislike

❑ Dislike   ❑ Strongly dislike

Please give reasons for your preference:

_____

_____

A Town Down Under

Meet the men of Paradise Creek, an Australian outback township, where temperatures and passions run high. These guys are rich, rugged and ripe for romance – because Paradise Creek needs eligible young women!

How much do you like this storyline?

❏   Strongly like   ❏   Like   ❏   Neutral – neither like nor dislike

❏   Dislike   ❏   Strongly dislike

Please give reasons for your preference:

_____

_____

The Marriage Treatment

Welcome to Byblis, an exclusive spa resort in the beautiful English countryside. None of the guests have ever found the one person who would make their private lives complete…until the legend of Byblis works its magic – and marriage proves to be the ultimate treatment!

How much do you like this storyline?

❏   Strongly like   ❏   Like   ❏   Neutral – neither like nor dislike

❏   Dislike   ❏   Strongly dislike

Please give reasons for your preference:

_____

_____

Name: _____

Address: _____

_____

Postcode: _____

Thank you for your help. Please return this to:

Mills & Boon (Publishers) Ltd
FREEPOST SEA 12282
RICHMOND, TW9 1BR

           NO STAMP NEEDED – postage has been paid.

2 FREE
books and a surprise gift!

We would like to take this opportunity to thank you for reading this Mills & Boon® book by offering you the chance to take TWO more specially selected titles from the Medical Romance™ series absolutely FREE! We're also making this offer to introduce you to the benefits of the Reader Service™—

★ FREE home delivery
★ FREE gifts and competitions
★ FREE monthly Newsletter
★ Exclusive Reader Service discount
★ Books available before they're in the shops

Accepting these FREE books and gift places you under no obligation to buy, you may cancel at any time, even after receiving your free shipment. Simply complete your details below and return the entire page to the address below. *You don't even need a stamp!*

YES! Please send me 2 free Medical Romance books and a surprise gift. I understand that unless you hear from me, I will receive 4 superb new titles every month for just £2.55 each, postage and packing free. I am under no obligation to purchase any books and may cancel my subscription at any time. The free books and gift will be mine to keep in any case.

M2ZEA

Ms/Mrs/Miss/Mr ....Initials.............................
                                                        BLOCK CAPITALS PLEASE
Surname ....
Address ....

....

....Postcode..........................

Send this whole page to:
UK: FREEPOST CN81, Croydon, CR9 3WZ
EIRE: PO Box 4546, Kilcock, County Kildare (stamp required)